Come On, Eileen

Stories

M. G. Stephens

SPUYTEN DUYVIL
New York City

Acknowledgments

Some of these stories have appeared in the following magazines, for which the author wishes to thank their editors:

"A Day in Court," "The Prodigal Daughter" and "Hampstead Road" appeared in *The Missouri Review*

"Skint" appeared in *Solstice*

"Sheltered" in *Notre Dame Review*

"Jazz at the Top," *The New Engagement*

ISBN 978-1-963908-66-4
Cover art:
Queens: The Philosopher. chalks, oils, charcoal on canvas, 22" x 26".
©Basil King 2010 Artists Rights Society New York (ARS).

Library of Congress Control Number: 2025934114

For Sage & Etta

Mine are the rouge pots,
the hot pinks,
the fledged
and edgy mix
of light and water
out of which
I dawn.
—Eavan Boland

That day I got into dire disaster.
　　　　　　—Edna O'Brien

Noli timere.
(Don't be afraid.)
　　　　—last words spoken by Seamus Heaney

SILENCE

"The only honesty is silence"
—Sinead Morrissey

A DAY IN COURT

The absent girl is
Conspicuous by her silence
Sitting at the courtroom window
Her cheeks against the glass.
　　　　—Eiléan Ní Chuilleanáin

Salisbury Square was just off of Fleet Street, and it had gone nine o'clock in the morning when Eileen arrived there for her hearing. She had been there a week earlier to drop off her skeleton argument with the Employment Appeal Tribunal, and that morning looked no different from a week earlier, except that day had been sunny and this one was pissing down with rain. This is where the old newspapers used to be printed, the streets filled with conmen, journalists, lawyers, and various hacks. The enormity of the rain did not stop a handful of people, probably solicitors, from speaking on their mobile telephones under big umbrellas. These men looked as rumpled and sleazy as characters out of Dickens' *Bleak House*. Talk about Jarndyce v Jarndyce, nothing had changed in this world in over a hundred and fifty years, although the tribunal itself was a product of the postwar era, instituted in a time when the working poor were given some legal rights. Eileen had girded herself as she turned the corner off of Fleet Street and came down to the square, and during that walk she had told herself not to be fooled or become overly optimistic. This was not a fair hearing. The lower tribunal had already dismissed her claim half a year ago, writing that she had no reasonable grounds to succeed with an appeal. This was going to be a formality, one last chance to make her point about what happened, and how the lower court's judgment contained errors of law. It was going to be her last aria. Eileen had the same thought entering the building that she had the week before: she was entering the graveyard of justice.

Even with an umbrella, she was soaked through because of the wind. It was June but it felt like December. Her hands and feet were numb with cold. She had worn flats, and they were soggy now, her stockings dripping wet too. Her dressy outfit was made of Irish linen, a birthday gift from one of her sisters. She had matched the dark blue of the linen suit trousers and jacket with a red silk blouse and a colorful scarf that she had purchased years ago when Santiago was still alive and they were living at the Hotel Lenox in Paris. Her cotton raincoat worked well in a drizzle but was worthless in this downpour, so that the linen suit was rumpled, as was the red silk blouse, making her look as if she had slept the previous night in her outfit. At least that was how she felt and how she thought others perceived her.

It was her birthday, and she had just turned sixty-five-years old. Happy *fecking* birthday, she thought.

At the front desk, Eileen had to sign a directory before taking the elevator to the second floor where the appeal tribunal courts were.

"I hope you enjoyed the summer we had last week for two days," the guard said.

He had an accent she knew, and from his face she guessed he was from Ghana.

"Apparently that is all the summer we will have," the other guard said.

She was a pretty Asian woman, with beautiful dark skin and long light brown hair.

Eileen did not fancy talking about the weather, and yet she knew that is all people would talk about this morning, so she grunted her acknowledgement to the two guards, shook herself off, signed in, and then went up in the elevator to the appeal tribunal.

She turned left off the elevator and walked down a hall until she came to a reception. She was greeted by a man wearing a white shirt and a tie who had a similar accent to the guard at the entrance. He was a big man, almost like an African warrior, and his smile was broad and friendly, even as he stood behind the thick protected glass window with a tiny slot at the bottom for handing over paperwork.

Eileen slid her paperwork along with her identification through the slot in the thick glass window.

"Good morning, good morning, it is quite a day, yes," he said. "Yes."

"I have a ten-thirty appointment with Judge Hourahan in Court 4."

"Are you Miss Ng?" he asked, looking down at his clipboard for the activities that morning in Court 4.

Eileen could see that she was matched up with two

other names, all of them scheduled for Rule 3(10) hearings at that hour in that court.

Eileen wanted to say: "Do I look like Miss Ng?" Instead, she shook her head: No.

"I know you are not Miss Kano," he said, "because she's already there. So you must be Miss Coole."

"I am," Eileen said.

He asked her for a different form of identification, something with her date of birth, and she slid her Irish passport through the slot. He examined it carefully, then he smiled broadly once again.

"Well, happy birthday, Miss Coole."

"Thank you," Eileen answered.

"Let's hope for a good birthday surprise for you today."

"Thank you," she repeated.

"It is some weather," he said.

"It is," said Eileen.

When he spoke, he smiled, and his smile reassured her. Eileen could not help but smile back. He slid her paperwork and identifications back to her.

"You have a beautiful smile," he said, "but I am being forward with you, and even if you were frowning, it is none of my business. Excuse me, Miss Coole."

He then pointed to his left and directed her to the door there. He would buzz her in, he said.

There were five courts along the right wall. On the left, as she entered, there were seating areas for each court, so Eileen went to Court 4's area and took a seat. In front of each court there were ten or twelve wooden chairs with red upholstery on the seating, the row broken up by low pale blond wooden side tables where people had spread out their papers. The wall that separated Eileen from the courtroom was made of opaque glass and white plaster.

It seemed more like a waiting room on a maternity ward in a hospital than a high court. Eileen imagined expectant fathers pacing up and down the gray carpet.

Both Miss Ng and Miss Kano were already there. Miss Ng must have slipped in without the guard seeing her.

"Are you lawyer?" Miss Ng asked.

"No," Eileen answered. "I am not."

"Are you criminal?"

"Certainly not," Eileen declared. "This isn't that kind of court. It's an employment tribunal."

"I know, I know," Miss Ng said impatiently.

Miss Ng wore a long bright red puffer jacket that was zipped to her neck. She had a bowl-like haircut, short and unfashionable, and she was not a handsome woman.

"Are you claimant?"

Her use of the word "claimant" was said in a heavily accented way that made it sound like something altogether different. But Eileen was able to suss it out.

"Claimant?" Eileen asked Miss Ng.

Miss Ng looked confused for a moment, then brightened up.

"Yes, claimant," Miss Ng said.

"Yes," Eileen said. "I am."

Well, at least they were not talking about the weather.

Miss Kano was sat taking it in, silent and demure. She

was a large African woman with a pretty face and she was dressed all in black, as if she were sitting in the outer room of a funeral parlor waiting for a service to begin. She smiled briefly at Eileen as if to say that Miss Ng was already putting her in a twist.

Eileen could not help noticing that all three of them were women. They each were scheduled to be in Court 4 at 10:30 a.m. A notice next to the door announced this information. No other cases were scheduled for that morning in Court 4. It was to be a festival of Rule 3(10) hearings, meaning that some benighted judge had deemed that none of these cases had a chance in hell of succeeding, so they would be thrown out after this oral hearing.

But why were there only women in the waiting area? Eileen wondered. Of course she already knew the answer to her question. If you stood up for yourself in the workplace, the chances were good that you were a woman being harassed in some manner or other. She also could not help but notice that while all of them were women, none was British. Miss Ng looked and sounded as if she were Chinese. Miss Kano looked to be from Africa, although Eileen had met women in Dublin who looked like Miss Kano, and they had brogues so thick, you could cut them with a cleaver.

Eileen herself was the wandering Celt from Dublin, but someone who left Ireland a lifetime ago, though living in London was a relatively new thing. She had wandered the earth, from America to Northern Africa, through emerging countries of central Africa, through China and the two Koreas, Japan and Singapore, Australia and New Zealand. But then she was married to a jazz musician, a famous one at that, and they went where the gigs were. In the final years of her husband Santiago Santa's life, they had lived in Switzerland and then in Paris, where he died. She had taken the Eurostar under the channel and moved herself to London. That was more than ten years ago and several jobs later.

Just the other day, walking on Marchmont Street in Bloomsbury, Eileen stopped to look in the sale bins in front of Judd Books, and she heard several men speaking the most exquisite Italian behind her. She had studied Italian and French at school and she knew that their accents were Tuscan, so she imagined that what these men spoke was Dante's *lingua franca*, replacing the old Latin that had dominated for centuries. Eileen turned and was startled to see three very tall African men wearing identical khaki trousers, blue sportcoats with gold buttons, and white button-down shirts. Their footwear was the only thing different on them: one wore plimsolls; another brown loafers; the third had heavy tan brogues. (She knew the latter because Santiago liked those shoes, and he would buy them when they were in London at Tricker's on Jermyn Street.) These three blokes were right proper gentlemen scholars in Bloomsbury. They had undercut the stereotypes that even Eileen Coole, so broadly travelled and educated, had somewhere deep inside of her. Why couldn't three young African men speak perfect Tuscan Italian? There really was nothing odd about it. Professional football was filled with black men who spoke Italian or French, and looked for all the world as if they had just stepped off a plane from Addis Ababa. Eileen had been to Addis Ababa with Santa; he had gone there, not as a musician, but as an emissary from the black diaspora, an American with a finely tuned sense of the injustice in his own country and abroad. Eileen had gone as his wife and companion, but also a kindred spirit. That is why Santa loved her, despite all his infidelities, despite his drug addiction and alcoholism. He had let her know that she was the one for him, not just because he found her beautiful and incredibly intelligent, but because her sense of kindness and compassion, her sense of injustice, was sublime, just as his own was, and everlasting, not to be trundled out at the right moment, but a constant flame in the belly. Santiago Santa used to say to people: "There can be no spirituality without a sense of justice." And Eileen had agreed with him. She favored such an interpretation of the everyday world. They were soldiers in the same battle for justice. That is what took him and, in turn her, around the world and throughout Africa. That sense of fighting injustice had driven everything they did together.

Once, many years ago, when Santiago was touring Europe, he was the opening act for Miles Davis. They found themselves in Paris. It was that trip in which they had discovered the Hotel Lenox, as Eileen was visiting sites where James Joyce had lived. Santa had gone along because he wanted to know more about the writer too. When they got to the Hotel Lenox, Santa rebooked their hotel from where they were staying near Montmartre to this more centrally located hotel. Once they discovered that he was Santiago Santa, their room was upgraded. They begged him to perform in their little jazz room one night, and Santa agreed. He would play late one night after his gig with Miles. They were thrilled for the association, so that whenever they stayed in Paris after that, they stayed at the Hotel Lenox, usually for free because Santa was also playing in the lounge at the hotel after his concerts.

On one of those nights, they were approached by a jazz critic who was also a poet and philosopher. Eileen could not remember his name, but then it popped into her head. His name was Jean-Claude Avignon. He was a friend of the singer Serge Gainsbourg. He asked Eileen and Santa if they wanted to meet Samuel Beckett, and Eileen answered of course they did. Apparently Beckett was also a big fan of Santa's music. Who wasn't in those days? So after the concert, the philosopher-poet approached them and they grabbed a cab and went across the river to a student neighborhood where Beckett lived.

They went to an all-night café where the Irish writer liked to hang out and play pool, smoking cigarettes and talking to his friends into the early morning hours. He had already won the Nobel Prize in Literature, and it seemed that the only time he had relief from the public was when he ventured out into late-night Paris.

The philosopher-poet introduced Santa to Beckett and

they shook hands, then Santiago introduced Eileen as he often did: "This is my wife, Cathleen nee Houlihan."

Beckett nodded, almost bowing ever so slightly, to Eileen.

Someone once told her that she bore a striking resemblance to Lucia Joyce, James Joyce's daughter, with whom Beckett had had a brief encounter. Eileen worried that he might see the resemblance and be repelled by her. But instead he smiled, welcoming her to Paris in his impeccable French.

Beckett took her hand and said: "Cathleen, *enchanté*. Welcome to Paris."

He spoke French with a strong Dublin flavor to it, something that Eileen was familiar with, as she spoke French the same way.

"*Ça me plaît enormement*," she said.

But as soon as she said it, she realized that perhaps it was better said of a meal than meeting a person, especially if that person was Samuel Beckett, the legendary Irish writer, a fellow Dubliner, both of them from the upper registers of Irish life.

Eileen said something to Santa across the table. It was really nothing. She was just getting his attention.

"You speak French with a Dublin twang," Beckett said, putting a kind of fake American emphasis on the last word.

"Well, I would, wouldn't I?" Eileen said.

"Where are you from?" he asked.

"Sandy Mount," she said, making Sandymount two words.

"Black Rock," he said, and then he fell silent.

Beckett's silences were greater and more proportional than his yattering. He looked spare. He spoke sparely. He wrote even sparer still.

Eileen took a big glug of whiskey.

It was early in the morning in Paris, most people getting up and going off to work.

They were winding down for the night, these nightowls like Santa and Beckett.

Several hours earlier Santa had been on stage, warming up a large concert hall in preparation for Miles Davis and a sextet. Santa had sat in a few sets with Miles too. The great trumpeter appreciated the way Santa played the piano. He was especially good at *comping* Miles, which is why the trumpeter asked him to hang around. Santa could *comp* and then he could go off into a brief solo when called on and leave a pool of emotions hanging in the air, like thick drops of rain that refused to fall to the ground.

Eileen was still young and beautiful. None of the ravages of drug addiction had settled into her bones and muscles, and lined her face prematurely. That was just around the corner. That night, high out of her mind, she was as vibrant as Cathleen nee Houlihan, the mythical Irish host of Yeats' poems.

But this was not a circle of men who noticed a young beautiful woman, so she blended into the night, almost invisible to everyone there, including Samuel Beckett who was busy listening to everyone speak to Santa about music and other artistic things. Santa tended to like to talk about art and literature in such a setting. Music was reserved for the musicians, in the day time, in rehearsal studios, where shop-talk was the order of the day.

Beckett could have been Eileen's father, both of them were so tall and thin.

"She's like a Giacometti," he said to Santa, nodding towards Eileen.

"She's more like a Jackson Pollock," Santa said. "In the rare moments where she's calm, she's like a Mark Rothko, deep and moody."

Everyone laughed, but not Beckett. He stared at her, and even stared through her, deep into her soul.

Eileen was in a foul mood all the sudden.

"My name is Eileen," she said. "I'm Eileen Coole."

Beckett seemed to be mulling over her name.

"Silent at the point where stillness comes to meet it," he said, quoting a line at the end of a poem in her first and only book of poems, *Green Chimneys*.

Eileen's mouth dropped open and the flies in the room could have inhabited that space.

"Bloody fucking hell," she said, amazed.

It was nearly time for the courts to open for business. All three women were about to face Judge Michael Hourahan in Court 4. The only thing they did not know is who would be first and who last and who would be sandwiched in the middle and which spot was potentially better than the other or were all these slots as damned as the next? Each had been told on the telephone by the tribunal that they might be given free representation from a pro bono lawyer's scheme, but so far no one had turned up. Each woman had a stack of papers in a bound folder, different parts of which had been underlined in yellow or orange or bright green marker. Colorful tabs stuck out from the edges of Eileen's paperwork.

If someone from a health charity were to take any one of their vital signs, they might become visibly alarmed. Blood pressure, pulse, heartbeat, everything ramped into overdrive. Eileen was spiky and hyped up, and a little bolshie. She did not sleep well the night before. She figured that neither did Miss Ng or Miss Kano.

They had entered and now were ensconced in the graveyard of justice, a rule 3(10) hearing by an Employment Appeal Tribunal, next stop oblivion. Months earlier, in the court's sift, they had been culled and then placed at this doorstep beside the graveyard of justice, with the judge declaring that they had no reasonable chance of succeeding. This is where the judges liked to scold you and chide you for your legal infelicities, for the amateur level of your legal paperwork. This was not a place for praise and to single out good work well done. These claims had no reasonable chance of succeeding, they had been told. Yet Eileen had done her homework, spending countless hours at the British Library as well as some local branch libraries, combing through law books. She knew that two judges had ignored her points of law, and that there was a case to be made. That is why she was there, looking for that one honest judge, a London

Diogenes. Eileen knew that her hearing would be brief if she didn't make her points succinctly and accurately, showing the judge the errors of law and hoping that he agreed to extend the process, maybe with a full hearing several months down the road.

Trouble in the workplace had brought these three disparate women to the doorstep of the graveyard of justice, sitting in their red cloth chairs outside of Court 4 on the second floor of the Fleetbank House as they nervously waited for the proceedings to begin.

Every once in a while a clerk in flowing black robes walked by; sometimes a clerk stopped to ask what courtroom they were scheduled for and Miss Kano in the politest voice imaginable or Miss Ng in her abrupt harsh voice would tell them Court 4. No one seemed to ask Eileen, though, as her invisibility was near universal, in Northern Africa, across Africa, in China, Ireland, the US, people just didn't seem to notice her anymore, even though she was so tall, so thin, and so brilliantly redheaded, the curls of her hair flopping everywhere. Invisibility was a double-edged K-bar knife, something that could be used effectively in the right circumstances. Being invisible at the level of an Employment Appeal Tribunal was probably desirable. Going to a job interview, her invisibility was a detriment. Eileen had suffered a detriment and an unfair dismissal from the university where she had worked. That is why she was sat there in the graveyard of justice.

Eileen's linen trouser suit was beginning to dry out and pucker, turning the suit into a dark blue mass of wrinkles.

She repositioned her soaking wet raincoat away from all the paperwork in her folder. Miss Kano gave Eileen a febrile smile and a nod, as if to say good luck. Eileen acknowledged her with a nod of her own. Between them was sat Miss Ng who now talked very loudly to herself. Eileen wondered if Miss Ng was crazy or just eccentric or none of the above. Perhaps she was as crafty as Eileen and Miss Kano. Papers were strewn all about Miss Ng, almost like this were a performance piece called "Ophelia's Day in Court."

Instead of fifteen minutes of fame, each woman had approximately a half hour of it in Court 4 in front of the judge. A half hour was an optimistic time frame, though. They might be in and out in five minutes or less.

Luck might favor the prepared, but neither luck nor being prepared was enough. The Tribunal did not favor the claimant but the respondent, not because the latter was prepared, but because they were the Establishment, and in Britain luck favored the established order, not the lone wolf, the renegade, the singular voice, or even three disparate women, each calling out for justice. Eileen was prepared, but she needed more than luck. She needed a miracle.

As Eileen sat there she saw that like a ward in lockdown at a mental hospital, there were windows here but none of them opened. There were doors, but they didn't seem to lead anywhere or they were locked. If a door did lead somewhere, Eileen would have taken one of those doors, instead of the one leading into Court 4 along this corridor in the graveyard. If there were windows that opened, Eileen Coole would have jumped out of one of them by now. Instead she was sat in the waiting area of the EAT, as it was called, in the high court, waiting for them to call her case. There was nothing to do until she was called.

GREEN CHIMNEYS

"Who in their bleakest hour has not considered Iowa?"
—Caitriona O'Reilly

In Paris, after Santiago died, Eileen thought of topping herself. She was not just thinking about it, she planned on doing it. The black dog—what Churchill called his depression—had her in its grip. She could not shake it. But how would she top herself, and why? The latter, the why of it, was clear enough. She had wasted her life with an unfaithful man. Now she was alone. Adrift. There was nowhere to go. Her husband was gone. She might go to some place like Margate and walk out into the sea, never to return. She could do that in Nice, too. Walk out into the surf, pockets loaded down, like Jacques' were, with stones, very Virginia Woolf, that. She could jump off a tall building. She might dowse herself in gasoline, like a Vietnamese monk, and light herself up in front of the Irish embassy, protesting border guards at the frontiers. She could jump, like Anna Karenina, in front of a train. Instead of Russia, she imagined herself in some place like Chicago, where the commuter trains ran on the left side, as they do in London. Like Jackson Pollock or the sculptor David Smith, she could drive madly in a car into her own oblivion or like Albert Camus, another car fatality. But was his suicide? Were any of them? She might, like

Jack Kerouac, run along a railway track until the heart burst. Was that how he died? Or was it in a chair, in a house, a can of beer in hand, watching television, suicide by boredom?

She could drink poison.

She could drink.

That would be a form of suicide; she could throw away her years of sobriety, more than ten years of it, and drink herself into a coma, never to return.

Night and day she would think of topping herself, then get distracted by a newspaper headline, a song playing on a shop radio, the taste of a buttery croissant with a delicious cup of coffee, or a baby in its mother's arms, crying so beautifully, Eileen would postpone the inevitable for another day.

Instead of suicide, Eileen saw her mother and father, imagining them coming to terms with this daughter who had been born on 16 June 1946, and she wondered what her parents would think of it, i.e., topping herself. Her father was dead, but his spirit was ever-present in her life, and her mother was still there, across the roiling waters of the Atlantic, in her bolt-hole in Sandymount. Her mother, after Eileen was born, had insisted that the child be called Eileen, after her own mother. But Eileen's father had other plans. He wanted to name her Joyce, after the Irish writer because she was born on Bloomsday. Nineteen-forty-six was auspicious because it was the start of the Baby Boom in America and elsewhere. But in Ireland, instead of expanding, the population was shrinking, so that

Eileen's birth was especially auspicious for her family and their big house in Sandymount. Eileen was the middle child. Her brother grew up to become a doctor, just like his father, who was a renowned Dublin consultant. Her sisters married well. Eileen was the problematic one, good in school, actually brilliant in school, but never, as her mother liked to say, "with a practical bone in her body." She was tall and lean, like her father Dr. Leland Coole, but there the comparisons stopped. All her life she had wildly curly, flaming red hair, and what her father called a Celtic nose (meaning big). Eileen came into the world and into her own being with pale freckled skin. That is what people remembered about the girl, her freckles, her height, her nose, her hair. Always the tallest person in her class at school, whether the comparison was made with the girls or the boys, it remained so until she was in her teens, when she was only taller than the girls. Because she was thin and long, she appeared frail, but in fact was "as strong as an ox," her brother said, and she had amazingly rude health. She was unathletic, and yet she enjoyed reading about sports in the newspapers her father read, and enjoyed talking about the country's rugby football team. She would take long walks around Dublin and elsewhere, never tiring. Her stamina, her determination, her quiet ferocity were legendary in her family. She enjoyed music, singing and dancing, all the elements of what people in Ireland called good craic. She loved the craic. She was often compared to a figure in a Pre-Raphaelite painting, a compliment that made her bristle. "I'm going to kill the next person who says I look like a Waterhouse painting," Eileen declared to her family when she was in her teens.

In more traditional households, someone like Eileen might have "a calling," i.e., become a nun and teach or, if a male, be a priest. But Eileen Coole was not the convent type. She did not appreciate the rituals and customs of Catholicism, finding it mostly to be superstitions dolled up in ancient traditions. God did not interest her, but she was intrigued by fairies, leprechauns, cluracauns and other assorted good people. She was spiritual, but not religious. She had no interest in science, so medicine was out, and did not care about business, so going to some expensive American business school or the London School of Economics (LSE) was off the table. She had no intention of becoming a corporate CEO.

Her mother asked Eileen what she wanted to be when she grew up, and Eileen answered the same way every time: "A poet."

"A poet?" her mother laughed. "That is not a proper profession."

"That's what I intend to be," she declared.

Eileen was eight years old.

But she was consistent, making that same response when she was 10 and 12 and 15 and 20 years old.

Besides excelling academically, Eileen studied piano up through university, often playing keyboards for various rock groups while studying at University College Dublin. But writing was her true love. Her early poems showed that Eileen had an ear for imitation, for Yeats, sometimes Kavanagh or, across the sea, Larkin. But even her immature poems won many prizes. At UCD, her poetry evolved into something more full-blown and mature. She was the first in the literary crowd to speak about Frank O'Hara, the American poet, and the New York School of Poetry. "No, love, there is no building, it was a bit of a send-up, you know, they were just taking the piss calling themselves that." She also told her friends about the Black Mountain poets; the San Francisco poets, Jack Spicer, Robert Duncan, and Richard Brautigan. Eileen walked around Dublin, carrying around a beat-up copy of the Donald Allen anthology, *New American Poetry*, as if it were a bible, and in a sense, it was.

After university, Eileen applied for and was accepted to Iowa. Her father was not best pleased with her choices, nor was her mother, nor any of her siblings.

"How will you support yourself on poetry?" her mother asked.

"I'll find a rich patron," Eileen said.

Then she put paid to the argument when Iowa offered her a scholarship, a full ride—free tuition, book stipend, medical coverage, a room with board at the uni, and even a small sum to travel to the American Midwest from Sandymount. Her family remained skeptical up to the day of her departure when a sister drove her out to the airport for a flight to London, then New York for a week, and onto Chicago, and a bus ride to Iowa.

Eileen was ready to prove all of them wrong, and their responses only steeled that resolve.

Ah, but these memories were all a load of bullocks. She was alone in Paris, the widow, the one left behind, and her dear husband, her partner of these many years—since she was in her early twenties, while now she was middle-aged, deep into her fifties—had popped the mortal coil without getting his life in order. After Santiago died, Eileen dreamed about him, not as the man she had known through her twenties, thirties, forties, and now fifties, but she saw him as a young boy in Brooklyn. These dreams were the result of Santiago's own stories about growing up in Brooklyn in the Twenties and Thirties, through those boom and bust years, though it was mostly bust for him and his mother. People said that he looked like his father Santiago Santa, Senior. He did not know his father. He lived with his mother Annie in a third floor walk-up apartment facing the El on Broadway. People called this part of the borough East New York, a place that most New Yorkers would be hard put to find on a map. He was a dark and handsome child and bright in school, and this was contrasted with his mother, who had red hair and pale skin, and who he thought was very beautiful, but who had only gotten an eighth-grade education. She could be harsh and rough, but he knew that she loved him. He tried to be obedient and to help her in any way that he could. Their flat had three rooms with the bathtub in the kitchen, the middle room. He slept in the backroom, she on the sofa bed in the front room. His mother called it the parlour. That made him laugh. His friends called it the living room. The rooms smelled moldy, the flat was often cold in winter and scorchingly hot in summer. The Irish and Italian boys in the neighborhood often gave him a hard time. He was called racist epithets, and he did not like being called the N-word, a word he detested from childhood right up to that moment he died in the Hotel Lenox in Paris. But it only made him more resolute to succeed in whatever it was he was meant to do in this life. He attended classes at Our Lady of Lourdes, only a few blocks away. Their apartment, his mother's and his, was near the Halsey stop on the El. He spent his childhood looking out the window—the same as his mother—watching the action on the street below. Every couple of minutes a subway train passed. Sometimes kids waved to him. Occasionally some adult gave him the finger or, if they were Italians, they flicked their hand outward from under their chin and mouthed the words, *Va fungu*. He did not know exactly what that meant, but he presumed that it meant something like, Go fuck yourself.

Once a teenage girl blew him a kiss from the train, and he blushed, turning away from the window.

Now he was in fourth grade because he skipped kindergarten, having already learned to read by first grade. At school the nuns praised him. He was well behaved, quiet, neat. He was also the smartest boy in the class. Two or three girls were smarter. A nun came by the apartment to speak to his mother Annie. His mother did that Irish thing and served fruit cake and tea to the teacher. They sipped their tea from chipped cups, none of which matched. They were sat at the kitchen table in the two chairs, one painted red, one yellow. The fruit cake was from Christmas a few months ago, a loaf that she had purchased at Einhorn's supermarket. It was the kind of cake that lasted longer than regular cakes.

"Is something wrong?" his mother asked. "Did he do something at school?"

Before the nun could answer, his mother turned towards Santiago, sitting on the couch in the parlour.

"If you did something bad, I'll crack your head with my fist. I'll personally sort you."

"He didn't do anything wrong," the nun said.

Normally his mother wouldn't have extra tea, milk, and cake.

She had just been paid by the factory where she did piece work, had gone to the store over on Rockaway Avenue and bought the tea and milk.

"Santiago has a gift," the nun said.

"And just what is his gift, sister?"

His mother seemed skeptical that her only son had a gift.

"Music," the nun said, smiling.

She taught music at Our Lady of Lourdes.

"I want to give your son piano lessons."

"We can't afford those sorts of things," his mother said.

"No charge," the nun said. "I'll give him an hour of personal instruction three times a week."

"I don't know," his mother said. "I'm not sure I want him doing that."

They were silent.

Santiago stared out one of the two windows facing the El and watched a Broadway train pass.

"More tea?"

"Yes."

His mother poured from the teapot. The nun sipped her tea from the cup, then nibbled on the fruitcake.

In New York, a distant relative, a cousin, let Eileen use her cold-water flat in the East Village, a half-block from St. Mark's Church in the Bowery, and it was in that Lower East Side neighborhood that she got invited to a downtown Manhattan literary party at an artist's loft on Great Jones Street, and it was there that she met the poet Frank O'Hara who introduced her to all his friends. It was June 16th, her birthday, and she was twenty years old, so O'Hara, taking her under his wing, introduced her to his friends, Kenneth Koch and John Ashbery, Mike Goldberg and Larry Rivers.

"It's Eileen's birthday," Frank shouted.

They all sang "Happy Birthday" to her, and she could feel her face blushing.

That was the first extraordinary thing. The second was meeting Stan Swanberger, a young downtown intellectual, New York City poet, Jewish, a student of the poet Paul Blackburn at the City College of New York, uptown in Harlem. Stan had long curly locks and a big black mustache like Groucho Marx, and no matter what book she mentioned, he had read it and had quite a bit to say about it. Jack Spicer? Read everything published to date, he said. Robert Duncan? He'd even read part of the H.D. manuscript, he claimed, and had read everything else, not once but several times.

He walked her home to the tenement flat on East 10th Street after the party. They walked up the Bowery until 9th Street, then cut over on a diagonal which put them in front of St. Mark's Church, which he explained was about to be the host to the new Poetry Project that would open in the autumn. Why was she going to Iowa? he asked. "Everything is happening here," Stan said. An old tramp asked him for a dollar, and Eileen was amazed to see Stan hand over the dollar to the tramp. "But for the grace of god," Stan said, and it endeared Eileen to him from that moment, not to mention that Stan seemed brilliant and erudite and was a practitioner of a craft both of them had in common. She invited him up. He produced a neatly rolled stick of marijuana when they got into the apartment, and Eileen smoked her first bit of pot in her life, and the next thing she knew, they were naked and fucking on the mattress in the living room, even though there were no curtains on the windows. But it was New York, and that is what people did in the East Village in 1966. That evening Eileen would gain some things, and lose some others. She would smoke pot for the first time and lose her virginity. She had met Stan Swanberger and the poet Frank O'Hara, whose *Lunch Poems* Eileen adored and, besides her virginity, she would lose her wallet, although it would show up later in the morning on a dresser in the back room of the tiny flat.

Stan was with her the entire week, taking her to poetry readings, afternoon art movies in Chelsea, evening meals in Chinatown; deep, rich coffee and rolls in an Italian coffeehouse on East 11th Street near First Avenue, long hours spent in the Eighth Street bookshop, perusing the poetry collection, pizza and falafel sandwiches, pierogi on Avenue A, and even meeting Allen Ginsberg in front of the building where she was staying, and much to her amazement, Ginsberg shouted out, "Hey, Stan, when are you going to come over and show Peter and me those translations you did of Mayakofsky?" Next week, Stan promised. "I'm hanging out with my friend Eileen Coole until she goes off to Iowa, Allen, I keep telling her that the Lower East Side is where poetry in America lays, but she's convinced it's out in the cornfields of Iowa. "Hiya, Eileen Coole," Allen Ginsberg said, "I like your hair. Where'd you get it?" Eileen laughed. "I found it on my head in Sandymount, Dublin, Mr. Ginsberg." Then he told Eileen that he had just been to Dublin to give a reading at Trinity College and afterwards he bought a tweed suit at Kevin and Howland's tailors on Nassau Street, "and dontcha know," he said, "I have already left instruction that I am to be buried in that suit." Eileen laughed again. "That's good craic," she said, and then Allen laughed.

Stan was already halfway down the block towards First Avenue and talking to a craggy, rumpled, older man at the intersection, so Allen said, "you had better catch up with Stan, Eileen Coole, and say hello to Wyston Auden for me."

"Wyston?" Eileen asked.

"Yes, Stan is talking to Wyston right this moment," and Ginsberg pointed down the block to where Stan was engaged talking to an older man with the craggiest face Eileen had ever seen. She said goodbye to Ginsberg and trotted off to Stan and his other friend Wyston. What the hell am I doing going to Iowa? she asked herself, but didn't have time to answer her own question because Stan and his friend were engaged in a metaphysical discussion about prosody.

Meeting Frank O'Hara was probably a bigger deal than losing her virginity. He would die less than two weeks later, run over by a dune taxi on Fire Island, where cars are not allowed, his restless ghost forever roaming the streets of downtown New York.

Outside the tenement where she had met Ginsberg a few days earlier, Stan and Eileen had their first big argument. He belittled her for leaving New York while it was in the midst of a literary renaissance, as he called it, and "going off to the sterile, academic life of Iowa City."

Eileen took exception to his characterization of Iowa.

She was about to get a taxi on First Avenue and go off to LaGuardia Airport for a flight to Chicago where she would stay for a day or two, and then take a bus to Iowa City.

Stan had told her that he was in love with her. Why was she leaving him for Iowa?

Eileen did not have an answer to his question.

"Iowa is stale and traditional," Stan said.

As Eileen drove in the yellow cab to the airport, she said to herself, Stan is not the one, though she had no idea who the one was and when the one would appear, if ever.

Stan was a fling.

But this was all fabulous shite. Eileen needed less nostalgia and more practical ideas about how to resolve her current dilemma at the hotel in Paris in the 7th arrondissement. She could not afford to live in Paris now that Santiago had died and his royalties were going to his daughter and ex-wife, and what was the point of it anyhow? It was Santiago Santa's idea to live in Paris, and so they did, for the last ten years of his life. And what a life it was. Despite her trying to put him out of her mind to concentrate on her living situation, Santiago crowded her mind, clouded it with his assertions.

Eileen saw a nun with a slight brogue, her name Sister Mary Regina, who was from Dublin; Santiago Santa had told Eileen Coole this story many times. She was his grammar school teacher, not hers back in Dublin, but underneath the el tracks on Broadway in Brooklyn. The nun had once told the class where she was from, then went around asking the children where they were from.

Brooklyn…Brooklyn…Brooklyn…Mayo…Palermo, Sicily…Naples, Italy…Galway…When it came to Santiago, he said, "Brooklyn."

"No, not where we are," Sister Mary Regina said. "I want to know where you were born."

"Brooklyn," he answered.

In the play yard during the lunch hour, a boy named Carlos said, "She expected you to say P.R. or Cuba."

"I know," Santiago said. "But I'm from Brooklyn."

"Me too," his new friend said, "though *mi madre y mi padre* are from P.R. Where is your father from, Santiago?"

"Havana," he said.

Santiago wasn't sure if he should tell Carlos about his grandparents. Carlos may not understand, Santiago figured.

"Does he smoke cigars?"

"Who?"

"Your old man."

"I don't know."

"How come?"

"I live with my mother."

"The lady with the red hair?"

"Yeah."

"Is she Cubana?"

"No, she be a white lady from Brooklyn."

"No Cubana?"

"Her parents—my grandparents—are from Ireland."

"You mean like Sister Vagina?"

"Yeah."

"Dublin?"

"Her mother."

"And your grandfather?"

"My grandfather came from Galway, north of it in Connemara."

Carlos sang: "How are things in Connemara?"

Santiago tried to punch him playfully, then the school bell rang and they lined up to go back into the classrooms, recess over.

"How are things in Connemara?" Carlos sang in a whisper to Santiago.

"Quiet, Mr. Lopez," a nun cracked.

They marched back into the school building.

Their class was filled with immigrant children, most of them Italians, with some more Irish, a couple of black kids, and then a handful of kids from Puerto Rico and Cuba.

The neighborhood was Italian, at least the shops on Broadway were—barber shop, butcher, tailor, grocery, bakery.

Santiago used to say that "one door closes, and another one opens." Occasionally he added: "Sometimes you wait in the hallway." Eileen was in the hallway. She had to make a decision about her life in Paris, which was coming to an end, and where she might end up. It was no easy decision. She liked Paris, but she was not sure she wanted it to be her home. She did not want to leave the Hotel Lenox feet first the way Santiago had. She wanted to leave via the door, suitcases in hand, trudging off to the next phase of her life. Widowhood was a motherfucker, she thought. Grief was a motherfucker. Even Santiago was a motherfucker. Everyone was a motherfucker, including herself, the biggest motherfucker of all. But instead of coming up with a solution for where she was to live, Eileen found herself sitting in a café, drinking coffee which she rarely drank—she preferred tea—and writing in her clairefontaine notebook with her yellow Lamy fountain pen, not about Santiago or what she was to do next, but of Iowa.

Eileen was at Iowa when she heard that Frank O'Hara had died. He was such an elegant fellow, she thought, and she cried. He was so young and handsome and such a beautiful poet. Eileen was not the crying type. One of her sisters called her the Ice Princess. Her mother once asked her if she actually had ever had a real feeling. Eileen laughed and stomped off. But she loved O'Hara's poetry, still in the after-glow of having met him in downtown Manhattan. Now she carried around a worn-out copy of his *Lunch Poems* in her knapsack, and would bring it out at a moment's notice. His poem about Lana Turner was her favorite. Her whole sense of Manhattan was filtered through his poems. He was the real deal, an Irish bard, generous and compassionate, loving and kind, and witty as hell, she would say when someone at Iowa had the nerve to ask her what was so good about Frank O'Hara. After a few of those types of encounters, she developed a low profile, moving under everyone's radar.

Her drinking escalated because she missed the craic in Dublin. She hung out in some dives where there were not too many students, and got to know some locals— all dedicated alcoholics—and a few graduate students with drink problems. One of them was Hugh Selwyn, another poetry student. He was tall and staunch, wearing tweeds, looking like an anachronism, a bit like he was the reincarnation of T. S. Eliot. Eileen wrote in a distinctly American open-verse style, but Hugh wrote poems out of 19th century England, as if the 20th century never occurred, and that Modernism was just an idea that hadn't bore fruit. Eileen thought Hugh was gay, and yet he was in love with her. His love was as formal as his poetry, never really declared or acted upon. He sat there, moony and unreal, drinking with Eileen, his Muse. They would drink at George's or some other bar. Hugh was a 22-year-old virgin, and he did not know how to progress their relationship beyond these drunken conversations which they had in the local bars, posh and dive, of Iowa City, and afterwards stumbling through snow, looking for Chinese take-away. Eileen had no interest in Hugh beyond his bar-room companionship. She didn't even like discussing poetry with him, as it was stilted and tight-ass the way he talked about Shelley or early Yeats. Her conversations with him consisted of sports (rugby football, hurling, and football, the Irish and British kind, not the American football). He was knowledgeable about 19th century fiction, and he was smart about practical things like where to buy household cleaning products, mops and brooms, toiletries, and paper products. Hugh became Eileen's poodle.

After a year in Iowa, Eileen was warned by her mentors that she was wasting their time because she wasn't committed to the program. If she didn't buckle down, she was going to lose her scholarship. Her grades were all right, but she had proved to be one of those talents that show potential, and then nothing more. That all changed when she had a poem published in *The New Yorker*.

An Old Woman In Dublin Reflects Upon Her Life

All summer she had been like an open
Wound, raw and unnerved, but soon that seemed to
Heal little by little, and she got on
With her life, doing more and more new things,
Meeting new friends, going to new places,
Trying to do things outside the comfort
Zone she had previously known, until
She was a person transformed by it all.

Sometimes she fell back into old habits,
And she paid dearly for this failure of
Imagination that put her right back
In that painful place where she had just been,
Taking back her will and return to
The old bondage of self, her diseased brain.

A short time after the poem's publication, she won a poetry prize that included publication of her book, *Green Chimneys*. Seamus Heaney had been the judge. In the announcement of the award, he spoke highly of her poems. Suddenly Eileen went from being the Irish goat, a scourge, to being everyone's favorite student; from near complete obscurity, drinking herself into oblivion in the dive bars with her accomplice Hugh Selwyn her only companion, she became a minor poetry star among the competitive graduate students. In the Poetry Wars, Eileen had become a general. She did not necessarily like her new status, as it made her feel even lonelier. So her drinking escalated, something she never had a problem with previously.

It was now late summer, just before Labor Day weekend, and already Hugh wore a blue blazer and had on a starched blue button-down Oxford shirt. He wore a rep tie. The crease in his khakis appeared to be cemented on with Krazy Glue. He wore a pair of brown, polished loafers with argyle socks. Eileen thought that he looked like a Jesuit on holiday.

They sat in a dive bar on the edge of town, one that they frequented when they wished to indulge in "serious" drinking.

"The Irish aren't alcoholics at home," she said. "We're just heavy drinkers. But when we come to America, we become alkies."

"I've heard something about that," Hugh confessed.

"Where?" she asked.

"From you."

"Oh."

"You've been floating that theory for some time."

"In America, if you say something enough times…"

"—and loud enough…"

"It becomes the truth."

"You've been saying that a lot too."

"I need new material, Mauberly."

Eileen liked to call him Mauberly when she was drunk. It was how Hugh could tell she was drunk; she would begin to call him Mauberly, after the Ezra Pound poem. When Eileen was very drunk, she called Hugh "a factitious trout," a misquote of EP's poem, or she would say that Hugh's Penelope was T. S. Eliot. Sometimes Eileen might venture beyond very drunk into a state more closely aligned with alcoholism, like a denizen in some Eugene O'Neill play. Then she ranted about not being "an adjunct to the Muses' diadem."

"What are you talking about, Eileen Coole?" Eileen cried.

"I need new material, Hugh."

"You need a vacation."

"Where to go?"

"California," he said. "Or maybe D.C. I'm going there for an interview next week. You're welcome to come along."

Eileen was still very drunk.

"I have no intention of sleeping in the same hotel room with you, Hugh."

He did not blink or even seem hurt.

"I'm not that sort of person, Eileen Coole. I'm your good friend."

Eileen noticed, even in this stupor, that she was becoming mean when she had been drinking.

"The only reason I hang out with youse is because you're the only one who can drink with me, bottle for bottle, glass for glass."

"And no other reason?"

"I don't like your poems."

There. She had said it. If Hugh had said the same to her, they wouldn't be friends anymore. But Hugh was cut from a different cloth and was made of stronger stuff.

There was a pause in which everyone in the bar was silent and the jukebox didn't seem to be playing anything.

Hugh said: "There is some shopping I need to do before going back to my room to study."

He stood to leave.

Eileen broke into tears again.

"I'm so unhappy, Hugh. I'm sorry. I didn't mean to hurt your feelings."

Hugh remained imperiously unperturbable.

"My feelings are not so easily hurt, Eileen. I know that I'm odd man out in Iowa, with the program, the students, and even with you."

"But I really do like your poetry."

"No, you don't," he said. "You clearly don't."

"I was raised on formal verse—Yeats, Kavanagh, Larkin, Auden. I was the only one who defended your right to write traditionally in that poetry workshop last week."

"True."

"So sit down, you silly cunt, and buy me an Irish whiskey and a short beer."

"You've had quite a lot already, Eileen."

"And to think I was beginning to soften on you, you old cunt. Now you're beginning to sound like me mother."

When drunk, Eileen reverted to this mock Irish brogue, something that was nowhere visible when she was sober.

Her speech became foul and slangy. Her Dublin accent was as soft as the summer's wind. Most Americans didn't even realize that she was Irish or if she were Irish, they thought she was of that hyphenated American kind.

"Let's get some Chinese takeout," Hugh suggested.

"You silly bitch," Eileen said. Then she rested her head on the bar.

But wasn't it Eileen Coole herself who was the silliest bitch of all?

Her poetry book *Green Chimneys* came out in her final year at Iowa, and she had endorsements from really fine poets, alternative and traditional, men and women, American and Irish alike. Even Seamus Heaney praised her, though not enough to write her a formal endorsement despite the fact that he had picked her manuscript to win the award. He told her that he did not give endorsements. "I'm grateful that you liked the book," she said. He did introduce her at a reading at the university, and later, in his cups, he called her "the real deal" and to her individually, "a good person," which she took to mean that he thought she was all right. At the party after the reading, he said to her, "Eileen Coole, what are you doing in Iowa?" She told him that she was finishing up her degree and then maybe she might do some teaching.

"But what are you doing here?" he asked again.

"I'm getting a fecking degree," she answered, being slightly drunk again.

Heaney smiled, stone faced, the great Irish sphinx, with

his Asiatic eyes of a Dionysos dissecting and x-raying her.

"You're a good woman, Eileen," he said again. "And a fine poet."

With that, his minders sheparded him away to meet more important Iowa people.

Hours later, many drinks down the line, he came back to Eileen. "It is a fine book," he said, "that is why I picked it from amid all the other excellent manuscripts."

"I'm grateful," she said, suddenly sober. "Thank you, Seamus."

She gave him a kiss on his forehead, being taller than he was. It was a bit like kissing God. He pulled away. He was after all a very prudish Irish and Catholic fellow, formal and publicly proper, even after a night of boozing or especially after such a night.

Heaney was like Titian, only Irish; he had no enemies, only admirers of different degrees and influences. It had been so his entire life. He was a blessed soul.

His host came over and suggested calling it a night.

Seamus said goodbye to Eileen, and left.

Eileen laughed.

She found Hugh Selwyn in the crowd of partygoers.

"Famous Seamus says that he liked my poems."

"What did he say exactly?"

Affecting a Northern Irish accent, she said, "It's a fine book and I admire many of the poems."

"Is that an exact quote?"

"As close as I can be after a night of roistering with the hoi polloi of literary America."

Hugh laughed.

Eileen did not recall Hugh laughing previously on any occasion or under any circumstances. She was chuffed to get him laughing at her craic.

But it was not Eileen Coole's life which had come ingloriously to an end; it was her late husband Santiago Santa. Instead of thinking of herself self-pityingly, she tried to picture her handsome husband as a young man, growing up with a single mother, another Irish redhead. He had done well in high school, though not as well as he had done in grammar school. But he had done well enough to get a full scholarship—a basketball scholarship—to Columbia in Morningside Heights, where he played point guard, though they didn't call it that in the 1940s, the war raining down upon the world in Europe and Japan. He was the playmaker, the guy who brought the ball up court, set up the play, and if no one was open, he would drive to the hoop or stop and shoot a set shot two-handedly. In the 1940s, everyone tried to copy the team-oriented, highly intelligent ball play of the City College of New York, a mile north of Columbia on Amsterdam Avenue. Santiago Santa was the essence of a smart ballplayer, hitting the open man, setting picks, dribbling everywhere, and then taking a two-handed set shot to score. At Columbia, he maintained his good grades and played basketball for four seasons. He formed a jazz quartet that often jammed at rent parties and in little clubs in Harlem, just down the hill from the campus. In Morningside Heights, he'd met

Allen Ginsberg and Jack Kerouac, William Burroughs and Herbert Huncke, usually in the West End bar, the student hangout across from the main campus on Broadway, where he would sometimes go to have a beer and talk politics and literature, his two favorite topics after music.

They were all smoking marijuana, but at the time he did not partake of it but once. It simply made him paranoid, so he didn't do it again.

He went down to the Village to play on the weekends, and he was introduced to various musicians, including Thelonious Monk (his hero) and Miles Davis (his friend). It was Monk who introduced him to everybody, including Charlie Parker, a man inspired by the divine fire of genius, or so Santiago said to his friends back at the university. At Minton's in Harlem, he met Dizzy Gillespie, and Santiago told him that Gillespie was his mother's maiden name.

"Maybe we're related, man," Dizzy said.

"At least cousins," Santiago offered.

"And I dig Cuban music," Dizzy told him.

"I dig bebop," Santiago answered.

"Yeah, bebop's way out," Dizzy said.

Santiago Santa set a record at Columbia for most points scored in a game. It was 47. Normally he got more assists than points, but no one was open that night, so he shot the ball. He scored. He was fouled and shot a free throw. That same game he did not miss at the foul line and scored 20 points from the free throw line. Afterwards, he said that evening was the greatest moment of his life, though a few years later, playing music in the Village, he couldn't even remember that night very well.

Or so he told Eileen many times as they traveled around the Maghreb and deep into Africa in the 1970s and Eighties.

Back in college, he wanted to play for the Knicks at Madison Square Garden. If he couldn't play for the Knicks, he would play for the Celtics. That would please his mother to know he played on a team named the Celtics. But that never happened. Instead, after Columbia, he wound up getting a Master's degree in music from Julliard.

After two years in the Army—stationed in San Antonio, Texas—he was given a dishonorable discharge. In the hysteria of the time, he was accused of being a communist because someone saw him reading Karl Marx.

Back in New York, he formed a trio with bassist Junior Jones and drummer Sonny Walters, who soon left to form his own group. That's when Carlos Lopez showed up. He was the same kid from the neighborhood when they talked in the schoolyard, and both were eight years old. Carlos had been in the Army, studied percussion at Manhattan School of Music, and now was a jazz drummer. They began to tour with Dizzy, Miles, and Monk at different times, travelling across the country in a beat-up station wagon, experiencing America as black musicians. They couldn't stay at most hotels, couldn't eat in most restaurants. In those days, you knew who might put you up in a particular town, and they often fed you a good meal. When the musicians returned to New York, it seemed that Santiago had blinked and now it was 1959.

He was a friend of the poet LeRoi Jones, and hung out

with him and their friends—the downtown poets and painters mostly. LeRoi and Santiago had both been thrown out of the military for being politically radical. Santiago re-ignited his friendship with Kerouac and Ginsberg and even backed up Jack a few times while the King of the Beats read from *Mexico City Blues* or some other book or manuscript. There were parties Santiago attended, where he might run into Roi, the painter Basil King, the poet Joel Oppenheimer, and see Monk across the room. These were wild parties, full of booze and people smoking dope, people in the corner going nuts, taking off their clothes as they recited a poem. Sometimes there were rent parties, thrown so that the occupant could pay the month's rent, and there would be a charge of five dollars at the door. It was great stuff, he thought. Then he would be off touring again, not to Europe and Africa yet, but just a few years away from doing that.

At the top of the Sixties, he went to Cuba with Roi Jones and a bunch of other like-minded people from politics and the university, to show their support for Fidel Castro. That came about when a political group asked him to accompany them to Havana. The group was called Fair Play for Cuba. On a personal note, Santiago hoped to find his father. He had only met him once, when he was still a boy. The old man had come to the apartment to say hello. He was a musician; he played the violin. He was delighted to know that his son played the piano. Santiago's father—Santiago Senior—played in an Afro-Cuban jazz band in hotels in Havana. He invited his son to come visit one day soon, and Santiago told his father that he would.Santiago asked around about his father. One of the Revolutionary soldiers assigned to the group—his name was Raul, just like Fidel's brother—considered the question, pondered it and said that Santiago's father was dead. Santiago Senior had died two years earlier, Raul said, not in combat or anything like that, but from a heart attack while playing in a hotel nightclub one evening. Raul told Santiago where his father was buried and invited him to go there with him.

On the day of the visit to the cemetery, Raul picked up Santiago and drove with him out of Havana into the countryside He was taken to the cemetery in the country, and it was there that Santiago laid a wreath for his deceased father. There were many highlights to the trip to Cuba—hearing Fidel speak out in the countryside to thousands of peasants, going to meetings with other young people, nearly all of whom considered Santa and his artsy friends retrograde American misfit rear-guard counter-revolutionaries, ignorant politically and emotionally naïve. The trip to the gravesite was different; he finally came to terms with his father, and thought that he could let his old man rest in peace forevermore. That was the best thing about the visit to Cuba.

As quickly as Eileen recalled Santiago's story, the self-pity returned, and instead of thinking of him memorially, she went back to feeling sorry for herself. That invariably brought her back to Iowa because her parents were never best pleased by her choice to go there. Eileen decided, as a way of getting in favor with her parents, to do a Ph.D. She applied to five places—Chicago, Harvard, Yale, Stanford, and Berkeley—and got into all of them. But she chose Berkeley because they offered her a good scholarship—Chicago also did too, but she didn't want to live any longer in the frigid winters of the Midwest—so she chose Berkeley. She also thought that she might be able to study with Seamus Heaney; but that did not work out. He went off to teach at Harvard. Still, Berkeley was considered the best English department in the country, and Eileen's dissertation would be Irish and feminist, drawing on lots of European ideas from France and Germany, so when she went to Berkeley that autumn, she felt more at home with the place than she did in Iowa, where she had felt like a mackerel out of water.

She found an old, restored Pashley bicycle and had some panniers and a basket put on it, bought a lock and chain, and was in business for her first semester on the West Coast. Her MFA from Iowa was under her belt, and it was a black belt in poetry. Her book of poetry was out in bookstores. One afternoon in North Beach, she went into City Lights bookshop and she held *Green Chimneys* in her hands the way a new mother might hold her infant child. She stared at the cover, read the poems aloud, wondered how it had happened. Reviews would be slow to come in, but they began early and kept coming in.

Eileen was quietly confident at Berkeley. Even her father would call her, full of parental pride, to tell her how good he and Eileen's mother felt about their daughter doing a PhD at Berkeley.

"You'll be able to put that one to good use," he said one mid-September afternoon when he called.

"It must be the middle of the night, da," she said, reverting back to her Dublinese. "You'll be waking the neighbors."

"To hell with the neighbors," he said. "This is Sandymount. I haven't seen the neighbor's in donkey's years."

She had never heard her father sound so positive. Over the years he had become more conservative, more dour; more or less fearful and resigned.

"Go on now," Eileen laughed.

"God's truth," he said.

"You're a wicked man, pa."

There was a pause.

"We are so proud of you, Eileen Coole."

Another pause.

He seemed choked up.

Again, it was so uncharacteristic of the man she had come to know as her bottled up and staunch and buttoned up father. He was so often a man of few emotions and fewer words, and what ones there were uttered, they were patina'd with his sarcasm. But now he did not seem to be able to continue; he was choked up.

"I'll put your mother on," he said, handing the telephone to Eileen's mother.

"Darling Eileen, how is the middle child?"

"The middle child is well."

"Ah, that's grand then. And how is California?"

"California sends its love," Eileen told her.

"Grand," her mother said.

This is a bit rich, Eileen thought. Since when had California become grand to her Eurocentric mother? While she lived in Iowa, Eileen had gotten used to her parents' constant disapproval, calling her rebellious, and her writing almost impossible to decipher. Neither parent cared for her poetry, which her father claimed was intentionally obscure and her mother said was above her job remit to understand. Her father was one thing, the rare Irishman who didn't care a tinker's damn about poetry, though he did like to boast, in his cups, that he had read all of James Joyce, not once, but many times. Her mother considered herself a literary cognoscente, telling her daughter of lectures she attended about Yeats and other luminaries of the Irish Literary Renaissance. The mother did not care for Patrick Kavanagh, though, "a bit too rough around the edges," she said. She liked T. S. Eliot, though her liking was more to do with Eliot's spiritual beliefs than his poetry. Though a good Catholic, Eileen's mother was a bit Anglican in her tastes.

Nowadays if her father read anything beyond the newspapers, it was Swift, and though he still professed to love James Joyce, he had not re-read him in many years. He did not care for O'Casey or Beckett or any of the modern ones. He read Shakespeare as a young man. He did like George Orwell's essays, but he did not care for

Orwell's politics. "Too leftist for my tastes," he said. He once read popular literature from America—Hemingway but not Faulkner or Steinbeck, O'Neill but not Tennessee Williams. His passion nowadays was for the opera.

In Dublin, Eileen's father was not only a prominent medical consultant, he was considered an intellectual despite his disdain for most of what they called Irish literature. Eileen could not fathom why her father was considered well read, when he was nothing of the sort. He had read Plato and Aristotle and he had made clever remarks about Socrates. His claim to culture was based on his reading philosophy when young, and going frequently to the opera with his wife. The night her father had called— her mid-afternoon in Berkeley—was the beginning of the new semester, and the week sped by without a moment to reflect. It was 1968, the Tet Offensive already a memory from earlier in the year, and the various deaths still acrid in the air. The death of Martin Luther King deeply troubled Eileen, and she wondered if she should continue on in America. Then came the assassination of Robert Kennedy, whose death had a sentimental effect on her, just the way the death of John F. Kennedy had affected her earlier in the decade. They were Irishmen, politicians, true, but also familiar figures out of her own history. The war in Vietnam seemed worse than ever in the autumn of 1968, but where Eileen hung her hat, in this part of California, the antiwar movement was as strong as it had ever been. There was some hope about the resistance, about the draft dodgers, the burning of Selective Service cards, while abroad in Southeast Asia, Buddhist monks were lighting themselves on fire.

The new university friends had suggested a night out before things got hectic with classwork and research. By Friday night, her university friends suggested going over to North Beach to hear some music at the Jazz Workshop. Thelonious Monk was performing.

Eileen had been told that Monk was erratic and might not even show up for the gig or, if he did, he might be hours late, so Eileen and the others got there around ten in the evening after a communal meal at a nearby hotel which specialized in French Provençal food. They paid a fixed fee and sat at a communal table with other diners, the restaurant of the hotel no bigger than a spacious dining room in some affluent San Francisco home. It was only a short walk to the Jazz Workshop in North Beach.

Someone named Santiago Santa performed as the warm up to Monk. With such a name, Eileen expected Latin jazz, but Santa's music was lyrical and progressive, inspired by Monk and Miles, especially the Miles of late, who was getting more electronic. He was no longer the Miles Davis of *Kind of Blue*.

When Santiago Santa's set ended, Eileen excused herself from the table and went to the ladies room. That night she was wearing what had become her American uniform—Frye boots, tight jeans, a linen blouse, a scarf, and a short brown leather jacket.

She had come out of the ladies room and stood near the bar when Santiago Santa walked out of the men's room and into Eileen.

He was trim, sleek, handsome, and slightly taller than Eileen's six feet height. He looked a bit like Albert Camus. A cigarette dangled from his mouth.

The drink went flying. He was quick to apologize.

"Don't be daft," Eileen said. "It was my fault, and I'm sorry."

"Dublin?" he asked.

"What?"

"Your brogue."

"I am nothing of the sort," she said.

"My mother was Irish."

"Your mother?"

"Well, not her. She was from Brooklyn. But her parents, my grandparents, my maternal grandparents. One came from Connemara, the other from Dublin. You sound like that one."

"Sandymount."

"She was North Dublin."

"I have to get back to my friends."

Eileen put out her hand to shake his.

"Great set."

"Thanks."

"See ya."

"Ta," he said, which made Eileen laugh.

After she was sat down, the waiter brought over a new round of drinks for everyone. He pointed to Santiago Santa at the bar.

Eileen explained to her graduate student friends.

"I literally walked into him," she said. "But apparently he's buying us a round."

She raised her glass towards Santa.

"Cheers!" Santa said, raising his glass.

"Cheers!" the others said.

Monk was supposed to have completed one or two sets by midnight, but he was still a missing person, a no-show, and nowhere to be found. Santiago did another set.

His music was full of sly improvisational twists and turns at the piano. He was backed up by a bass and drums, and yet this sound seemed to come from a much larger band.

Around one o'clock Monk showed with a Countess and some friends. Santiago was now sitting with Eileen and her friends.

Moments earlier Eileen had told Santiago Santa that her name was Eileen Coole.

"How cool is that?" he said.

At one point, while Monk played a solo, a tremblor rolled through the room, and the place seemed to tilt, sending Monk's drink flying across the piano. But he grabbed it just before it rolled off, took a sip, put the glass down, and went on playing.

"Talk about cool," Eileen said, and Santiago laughed.

After walking around Paris in a funk, Eileen headed back to her room at the Hotel Lenox. In the lobby, her mobile phone rang and she answered it without noting who it was. It was Carmel, Eileen's oldest friend. Carmel was grieving too; her husband Jacques, a journalist for Channel 4 News, had topped himself, walking into a pond at Hampstead Heath in North London, his body not found for days. Eileen's friend had just had a major show of her paintings mounted at a gallery in London. Eileen had to pull herself together and forget about her own problems for a minute, while she listened and commiserated with her old friend. Before Carmel's call, Eileen had been stewing in her own soup of self-pity, her bones marinating in the broth. Memories were one thing, and Eileen's memories comforted her to some degree. But memories would not find her a place to live in Paris or a job or a suggestion of what city she might settle into or what kind of profession she might engage. All of Santiago's royalties had disappeared. Eileen would have needed to be in New York for a court date to challenge those assumptions, and unfortunately that time had already come and gone. As Eileen stood in the lobby of the Hotel Lenox, that is when Carmel called her. It was a long story. These things always are. Suicide was less about despair and more about having no more choices. Once she spoke on the telephone with Carmel, choices suddenly appeared for Eileen Coole.

"Why don't you hop on the Eurostar and come visit me for a fortnight or two?"

"Brilliant," Eileen said, without thinking about it at all.

The next thing she knew she was going through the tunnel under the English Channel and was pulling into Waterloo Station just under two and a half hours later. She found the Edgware Branch of the Northern Line and took the Tube up into Hampstead, getting off in Belsize Park, and then walking down Pond Street into South End Green and out Agincourt Road onto Savernake Road and several minutes later, Eileen Coole found herself knocking on Carmel de Jong's door.

As she waited for Carmel to answer the knock, Eileen had no idea that she would not return to Paris, and that London was to become her home.

"Eileen Coole!" Carmel shouted, throwing her arms around her dear friend, kissing her cheeks, holding her tight.

Tears flowed down Eileen's face.

"Everything's going to be all right," Carmel said, as she escorted Eileen into her front room parlour. "No worries."

"No worries," Eileen repeated the refrain.

"Tea?" Carmel asked.

"I thought you'd never ask."

They laughed and hugged each other again.

Eileen remembered thinking, All is well, and all is well, and all manner of thing…

"Milk?" Carmel asked.

"A splash."

"Now I remember," Carmel said. "How long has it been since we saw each other?"

"Donkeys," Eileen said.

"Yes, donkeys," Carmel agreed.

JAZZ AT THE TOP

"Could it have happened, he wondered, at any other
time except the 1960s?"
—William Trevor

Leaving the Waterloo Station: it was an express, stopping only in Clapham before it shuttled down the
tracks to Surbiton. Twelve minutes from start to finish.
Eileen alighted from the train and tapped out at the gate,
then stepped down the long set of stairs to the exterior of
the station where black cabs queued, waiting for passengers. She only had to walk a short distance to Surbiton
University, where she taught half-time, and so she hoofed
it down the street in the direction of the campus. Her
walk was rapid and her long step covered great patches of
ground as she strode almost like a general reviewing the
troops, with great focus and command. A knapsack on
her back, she also carried two shoulder bags filled with
books. Eileen was nothing if not a beast of burden. In
two months, she would be sixty years old, but age was
relative, she thought. She had been to hell and back, so
this journey towards old age and death was almost a piece
of cake—a walk in the woods. Tall, she was even majestic
like a gazelle or like a Masai warrior, only a white woman,
and as thin as a pound sterling coin, her hair still quite
red, even with the gray streaks throughout, and the hair
was permanently set since childhood into a kind of Celtic

Afro, making Eileen appear like a deranged Orphan Annie.

She did not mind if people compared her to Orphan
Annie (her description of herself). It was those
comparisons to frail feminine creatures out of the pre-
Raphaelite paintings that put her knickers in a twist.
Derangement had its advantages, she thought, while
sentimentality was a pure and simple rot.

As she approached the Waitrose, she reminded herself
to stop there on the way home. She needed soy milk, tea
bags, bread, butter, toothpaste, deodorant.

It was only five years earlier that Eileen had wound up
in Waterloo Station, a widow, on the Eurostar train from
Paris to London. She even received the Irish welcome.
Two Special Branch operatives had separated her from
the queue and asked her to step into an isolation room
off the main lobby of the station where they proceeded to
interrogate her for close to an hour. They wanted to know
what she was doing in their city. "Like you," she said,
"I'm an EU national." That EU national blather put their
boxing briefs in a twist. An IRA bomb had gone off two
days earlier in Fulham. "I'm a citizen of the world," Eileen
said, "and I haven't been in Ireland for donkeys' years."
One of the security people snorted. "A citizen of the world
or an EU national, which one is it, Miss Coole?" Though
her arms and legs were dimpled with track marks from her
years of drug addiction, she had not practiced her defects
in more than a decade. She held her tongue. Eventually
they let her proceed onwards into London proper, another
older Irish woman looking for food, shelter, and work.

Being new to the academic game, Eileen had to work as if she were a young adjunct, not a woman fast approaching retirement, and when she was not teaching at Surbiton University, she was in Colchester, completing a doctorate in American studies at Essex University, having abandoned her studies almost forty years earlier in Berkeley. She and Santiago had lived for years in Algiers, where Santiago was well loved in the Maghreb and elsewhere in Africa, a legend, they called him, *sui generis*, the Nelson Mandela of jazz, they said, a man of conscience, a man of improvisational genius, someone with a strong sense of social justice, which counted for a lot in those days in Africa. The Islamists could care less about his music, but they respected his sense of justice and his masculinity, neither of which was ever in short supply.

Her colleagues at Surbiton University hadn't had anything like Eileen's experiences in the world, so she kept a lid on that part of life when she was around the academic community in London. She did sense that some of them resented her for empirical journeys beyond the cotton-wool cocoon of academia. None of them had travelled quite in the ways that Eileen had. She did not hold their lack of experience against them, but she was aware that some of them held Eileen's experiences against her. It was as if Eileen was just too worldly for them. None of them had transited the Sahara as Eileen and Santiago had, being guided to safety by Touregs. None of them had drunk palm wine at an oasis. None had drunk rot-gut whiskey with a North Korean dictator or been threatened to have their passports confiscated in South Korea by over-zealous CIA agents. None of them had lived their lives at the edge of the abyss, having survived a twenty-year heroin addiction or if they were alcoholics, were they capable as Eileen had been to admit their disease so openly and to seek help in arresting it.

Back in the day, their house sat in the hills, in a neighborhood near the university. All about the property there were olive trees, cedars, conifers, juniper, evergreen, and even an oak. There was a fig tree near the patio which looked out onto the Mediterranean below. The smell of eucalyptus was in the air, palm trees lined their street, and there was a grape arbor in one part of the garden. Scorpions and snakes lurked in the shrubs. The sky was a cloudless blue; the houses were so white, inside and out, forcing you to wear sunglasses outside because of the glare. The glare from the sunlight at noon made it almost impossible to see. North African sunlight was so intense, it seemed to make her blind when she looked at either the white buildings or the blue sky. Day's heat crept up on you; you needed to do things early in the day or else it became too hot to do them. They got up early and often sat on the patio drinking tea (Eileen) or strong coffee (Santiago). He smoked; she didn't at first, then she inexplicably began the habit after taking up running. Often they went to Tangier, and someone came from Algeciras on the night boat, bringing her oatmeal that Eileen would cook for them to eat at breakfast. The oatmeal probably originated in the British community in Gibraltar, right next to Algeciras. The trees and shrubs around the patio were muted, almost silvery greenish-blue in the daylight, so she turned her attention towards their presence in the cityscape. A dove sang mournfully on the wire near the white one-story building where they now lived. Lizards scurried at her feet or flicked off to the edges of her dreams or ran up a palm and circled out of her sight. She was more often thirsty than hungry in this tropical world, simple pleasures all that she seemed to crave, linen clothing next to the skin, light shoes on her feet. Gray storm clouds either massed in the valley below or banged up against the far hills, threatening rain off the sea. She did not walk alone as much as she used to, but found herself waking before sunrise, going into the big room and stretching, doing some yoga, other exercises before the sun or the staff appeared. She kept a notebook and often wrote after she stretched and exercised, again, before anyone who worked for them arrived or awoke and came out of their quarters. It was just such a day as this one that Santiago came out of his studio in the back of the big white house in the hills overlooking Algiers. He sat down at the round table on the patio and he lit a cigarette and stared off into space as he did a thousand times previously. They had been in Algiers for a while, their routines set. He slowly began to tell Eileen about a day in Oakland about six months before they met at the Jazz Workshop, and more important, why the Oakland police and the FBI so fervidly hunted him throughout the known world.

"You have asked me," he said, "why the police, the FBI, and now the CIA are so interested in me. Well, superficially, I associated with a lot of people in Oakland about whom the police had an interest, including Eldridge, Huey, Bobby, all the usual suspects in the Black Panthers. It was no secret that I was sympathetic to the Panthers. I donated money to them. I lent them support through my concerts. We were all very tight with each other."

Surbiton's Waitrose was one of the best one's in London. But Eileen had no time to go into it. Instead she sped up her pace towards the uni. For whatever reason, she was not in the southwest of London, but back in Algiers, sitting on that big patio which overlooked the city below and the Mediterranean Sea off towards the horizon and the desert to the south—that vast stretch of sand the size of Europe. Santiago Santa came out on the patio, smoking a cigarette, wearing a light-colored linen suit with sandals, and a sheer black tee shirt underneath the suit. He was already in his fifties, but he could have passed for half that age. He carried a small espresso cup, from which he sipped his morning coffee. It was one of those rare periods in which he was being faithful and neither of them was strung out on drugs. They had just come back from a successful tour of Africa, giving concerts in the Ivory Coast, Nigeria, Mali, Tanzania, Kenya, into the Congo ("the heart of darkness," he laughed but then said, "the real heart of darkness is the mouth of the Thames River where Conrad's story begins, that's the heart of the heart of darkness"). They were relaxed, him smoking another cigarette, she having a glass of wine, which was getting harder to find each day, as revolutionary Algeria was even more puritanical, if that were possible, than Ireland.

"You know our first visit to Cuba together was not my first visit there. I went there with a group called Fair Play for Cuba, along with LeRoi Jones and some other New York intellectuals and political activists. It was 1961. Roi was my good friend. I loved his poetry and his plays, his essays and his fiction. There was no one quite like Roi. He was an encyclopedia of music, not to mention his knowledge of literature. And he was small and ferocious, like a terrier. Some people's ferocity scared me, but not Roi's. His ferocity was beautiful. He was like Henry Armstrong or one of those great little boxers. Miles was like that too. Little guys, but they could knock you out just by looking at you."

Santa stared off into the horizon again, as if searching there for some answer to explain the incongruity of his life and how he wound up on this patio overlooking the Mediterranean Sea and these surrounding white houses and buildings in the hills of Algiers. A gray haze sat upon the sea. The heat was already building through the morning light. He smiled and shook his head.

"Roi later wrote an essay about the experience. He called it 'Cuba Libre' and *Evergreen Review* published it. It's one of the best essays I ever read, the others being

Jimmy Baldwin's 'Notes of a Native Son'; and his sermon, 'The Fire Next Time.' But Roi's essay on Cuba was a motherfucker. And his *Blues People* was a motherfucker of a *book*." (He now pronounced the word *book* the way his wife Eileen did, which was Dublinesque and memorable.) "They should make people read *Blues People* as part of becoming American citizens. That may be one of the most important books of the twentieth century. But 'Cuba Libre,' I loved that essay, and I was part of it too; I was there with him experiencing what he wrote about. Roi got all the facts right; he was a first-rate journalist, besides everything else he was capable of doing, including starting a revolution in America."

Santiago went on to tell Eileen that the trip to Cuba was a *motherfucker* too, and she understood that to mean that it was a great experience. LeRoi had given a poetry reading to thousands of Cubans massed to hear him. Later, Santiago played for them, something he always dreamed of doing one day, especially as his absentee father was from Havana.

"But I had no illusions about what was happening," he said. "The other left-wing delegates from around the world who had come to Cuba to celebrate the Revolution, they thought all the people from the US delegation—Roi and me and the others—were a bunch of rear-guard, lower echelon rear-area motherfucking reactionaries. They thought that we were only paying lip service to revolution, not sincerely dedicated to its devolution."

When the US delegates returned home via Canada,

they were hassled at Idlewild Airport in Queens on Long Island. Santa's phone was tapped. At the time, he had a railroad apartment on 10th Street in the East Village as it was just then beginning to be called. His mail was opened. The IRS audited his taxes year after year for the next decade.

And yet he was an upstanding guy, an idealist, and he had that strong spinal reaction to injustice. He bristled and then he dug in. He learned that from his mother. It was his mother who had taught him that strong sense of justice, and it was to characterize everything he did, and was the reason why his music had so much integrity and ideals—so much spine and guts, but also lyrical beauty to it.

"Without justice," Santiago Santa liked to say, "there is no spirituality. Without justice, there is no peace."

Other than his Fair Play for Cuba experience, Santa did not have any run-ins with the law; everything about him was kosher. Even his sidemen used to goof on him because he was so straight and earnest, and early on at least he did not take any drugs or particularly drink too much or mess around with a lot of women, although gradually all of that would change. He would snort cocaine, shoot heroin once in a while, drink until the wee hours of morning, and sleep with every woman he met. But he still was not in trouble with the law.

Eventually, even with the Fair Play for Cuba people, he fell off the grid and he went back to playing his gigs, being a jazz musician and composer who liked to mouth off about the injustice in the world, of which there was a great deal in the 1960s in America. In between numbers, Santiago Santa was known for talking about social injustice. Critics compared his banter between pieces of music to be akin to things that Nina Simone said when she performed. Sometimes he was on a bill with her and others, and the reviewers invariably talked about how similar their outrage was, and how devoted both of them were to social justice in the world. He drew many people to his shows because of his opposition to the established order, especially the Vietnam War, which he did not consider business as usual, but rather an aberration of justice.

Harry Belafonte came to his shows. So did Benjamin Spock; Peter, Paul, and Mary; even Bob Dylan. He was also friends with Dorothy Day and sent money to the Catholic Worker in downtown Manhattan.

"If she becomes a saint," he said, "she'll be the only saint I ever knew and also kissed."

The Black Panthers from Huey Newton to Eldridge Cleaver called themselves his friends. Santiago was their brother.

It was Eldridge who told him one night in Oakland, if the law came after you with trumped up charges, "flee into Mexico, go to Cuba, fly to Algiers."

It was a delightfully simple equation. Flee. Go. Fly. Mexico. Cuba. Algiers.

It is just what Santiago did around the time of the student killings by the National Guardsmen at Kent State

University in Ohio and shortly thereafter the killings at Jackson State. "We're putting Eldridge's plan into effect," he told Eileen.

"Bloody hell, Santa," Eileen had said. "I haven't even had a proper cup of tea this morning."

Santiago stood outside Jazz at the Top, smoking a cigarette and talking with some sidemen. This was half a year before he was to meet Eileen. It was late in the evening, and he'd already done two sets with one remaining. But it was summertime, the living hot and humid, and August's air was so thick, you could cut it with a razorblade, more like the East Coast where he had grown up than California, where he was, specifically Oakland, doing a gig near where he lived for so many years.

He was schmoozing with a bunch of musicians outside the club.

"I was playing with Charlie Mingus," Santiago Santa told the musicians around him, "you know, a great bassist, a great composer, a brilliant person. But Mingus was a moody motherfucker. We were standing like this, only outside the Five Spot in New York after it moved to St. Marks Place. Mingus had kicked the sax player off the stage, some young guy from Harlem. He didn't like the way he was playing Charlie's music. He got rid of the drummer. Didn't like what he was doing either. Mingus shouted at the audience. Called them rude ignorant white motherfuckers. He was like a man on a rampage. He was like a man on fire that night. I was expecting any moment that he was going to shit-can me. But he didn't. He said: 'Motherfuckn Santiago Santa, he knows how to comp and he knows when to take a solo and for how long…'"

Outside of Jazz at the Top, the group of musicians stood around listening to Santiago Santa reminisce.

An Oakland police car pulled up.

Two white officers got out.

Some of the sidemen nodded hello to the cops, but the cops didn't return the greeting.

Oakland had been seething all summer long, riots here and there, outbreaks of violence, police brutality, the usual shit during a heat wave in summer.

"Let's move along," one of the cops said.

Santa wore his trademark ivy-league suit, in this instance, a linen one, three-buttoned, with a white shirt and a colorful tie, loafers on his feet, looking more like a lawyer or a professor of philosophy at Columbia University than a renowned jazz musician.

Santiago caught the cop's attention and pointed towards the doors of Jazz at the Top.

"I'm doing a gig there," he said. "I need to go back inside to finish my set."

"Move it," the policeman said, shoving him.

"You can't push that man," one of the sideman said. "That's Santiago Santa. He's doing a gig here tonight. He's the main act."

"I don't care if he's Mahatma Gandhi," the other white cop said. "Move!"

Santa didn't say anything but moved along with the

others. And yet the two cops were not happy. They probably expected something different, some resistance, the way other knots of young men on corners had resisted them all through this week of heat and riots. There had been shootings, lootings, the summer shit show in the ghetto. The young men were restless and irritable throughout the city, but Santiago and his band members were not young men. They were middle-aged Black men. But that didn't matter; the police treated them as if they were teenaged boys.

At the corner, away from the glare of the neon lights from the night club, the first cop pushed Santa harder.

Santa knew the drill. He was from Brooklyn. You did not talk back to cops. You offered no resistance. That's what Reverend King had instructed them to do. Santa was in his forties, hardly a kid anymore, the rebellion bled out of him, though he was still strong and could resist if he wanted to. He figured that when the cops left, he would circle back to Jazz at the Top and finish his last set, no big deal. It was nothing new.

Santa was a tall, trim, athletic man. He was an inch or two taller than the two cops and certainly he looked to be in better shape than either one of them.

The first cop spun Santa around and hit him quickly on the side of his face, and Santiago went down, not from the force, but to make the cop think the punch was that powerful. Santa had moved with the punch, so its impact was lessened. He had boxed as a kid in the local gym in Bedford-Stuyvesant, even winning a couple of trophies, though he was never willing to take it further into the Golden Gloves. Fighting was not his thing; music was.

Santiago thought, reasonably enough, that that would be the end of it.

The other cop came over, spun him on his stomach and put his hands behind his back and handcuffed him.

Santa's face ground into the pavement, leaving a raspberry on his cheek.

The two cops pulled him to his feet, his suit ripped, blood running down the side of his face.

With his hands behind his back and handcuffed, Santa had no defense.

The second cop took him to the patrol car in front of the club.

The white owner of Jazz at the Top, Max Isenberger, a bald, fat, little guy with an intense Bronx accent, was outside arguing ferociously with the cops, after first trying to reason with them. These two cops were in no mood for conversation.

One of the cops shouted for people to break it up, keep moving, while the owner shouted at the cops that they would not get away with this shit.

They booked Santa for resisting arrest, loitering, and assaulting a police officer.

The news was in all the papers the next day.

Eye witnesses told reporters what really happened.

Both *Ramparts* and *Rolling Stone* magazines had long articles about it. The *San Francisco Chronicle* ran an article too, and so did the *Washington Post* and the *New*

York Times. The *Village Voice* compared it to the assault on Miles Davis by police in front of Birdland in Times Square a decade earlier.

Several days after he was arrested, Santa made bail, never having been in trouble with the law. His stint with Fair Play for Cuba was the only time his life drew law enforcement attention, and in that instance he was not breaking the law but practicing his right as an American citizen to affect alliances with like-minded people throughout the world.

A lot of people were upset with the Oakland police, not just about Santiago Santa, but about how they were treating members of the Black Panthers, who had originated on Oakland's streets. The Panthers ran food pantries and pre-schools, taught reading and writing, and to be a Black Panther, you agreed to read for at least two hours every day. Reading for two hours every day is what attracted Santiago Santa to the Panthers in the first place. They were revolutionary because they were so literal and commonsensical.

The Black Panthers had picketed in front of the courthouse during Santiago Santa's trial.

Neither policeman showed up for the court hearing.

Eventually the case was thrown out.

As Eileen walked through Surbiton past a pocket park and a series of modern townhouses that sometimes she fantasized living in, she did not think about her lessons that morning at the university, her students and their papers; the petty bickerings between her and her two line managers and her colleagues, all of whose *raison d'etre* seemed to be to thwart, even destroy her. When Eileen was a student at UCD, Iowa and Berkeley, she never realized how petty academics were, all of her experiences being so positive back then. Her mind naturally drifted away from where she was—nearly on the threshold of the university—and found herself going back to another time. Now she found herself back in the Maghreb, sitting on that patio, the only place where she found solace in Algeria, and could almost sense her beautiful husband talking to her, reminiscing about his life, the people he had known, the places where he had been, all of it reduced to this exile in Northern Africa, and the great continent to their south the place where they could move freely. Several times they hired a driver and took a Land Rover into the desert, sometimes going from Algiers down into the rural expanses of Algeria, out into some oasis where they ate dates and bread, going from Berbers to Touregs in the desert.

Sometimes the desert in the Santas, they floated above it all in a bed in Tangier. They simply dreamed the desert, and it was there, dry, deceptive, haunting, eternal, unfathomable as it was without beginning or end, the middle everywhere, sand shifting, dunes rolling up and down like waves in a sea, the intensity of the blue cloudless skies and the tawniness of the landscape, speckled occasionally by a palm tree. The edges of the desert were nowhere to be found; you believed in them almost as if it was an act of faith. It was both spiritual and spiritless.

The heat deceived them.

They thought they could handle it.

But no one can handle it, not even the nomads who simply endured it, but never simply handled it.

There was nothing to handle.

You picked up the sand and it drifted out of your palms in seconds.

A life was not unlike those grains of sand, running through one's fingers, there one moment, and gone the next. Once the sand had run out of her hand, Eileen felt the heat in her palm, even though there was nothing there anymore.

A headache came on.

Eileen often got headaches in the desert.

It came up gradually, then it possessed her.

Eileen was nearly at the doorstep of the university in Surbiton. Once again she felt almost as if transported back to Algiers. It was not so much a memory as it was a kind of flashback, a moment of post-traumatic stress, the way a combat soldier might recall his or her moments in the war. The walls were white, both inside and outside of the building, and this dizzying white was made even more intense by the sunlight, the cloudless skies, the vast blueness of the sky's dome, contrasted by the intense colors of the trees and bushes at certain times of the year, the bougainvillea, the grape arbor, the olive trees, the pines. Often she asked herself: is this what life is all about? Each time she asked herself that question, she got the same answer. This is what life is all about. Nothing more? Nothing. Is this what we were here to do? Was she fooling herself? This is what we are here to do; this really is what life is all about. The smell of the desert on the wind, the smell of the sea mingling with it, had twisted her brain. Where was she? But then a double-decker bus on the outskirts of London honked its horn as Eileen absent-mindedly crossed the street in front of the university. She came back to London, where the day seemed bleached of any color, where it was cool and damp and raining just a bit, enough to bring her back to this other moment, where she was going to work, making a living, and now living alone, her husband gone, Northern Africa gone, her need for drugs gone, alcohol gone from her life. She walked towards the front door of the main building, ready to meet her classes, ready to do her work, ready to survive in this foreign land.

Eileen remembered what Santiago used to call London: the heart of darkness.

EXILE

"Perhaps home is not a place but simply an irrevocable condition."
—James Baldwin

SKINT

When Eileen was hungry, Kilburn High Road looked like manna, especially the food shops. An Irish builder once said to her that if the British gave them back Northern Ireland, the Irish would return Kilburn to them. But that was a lifetime ago when Kilburn was London's Irish ghetto, just like Camden Town once was. The playwright George Bernard Shaw was so disgusted with his fellow Irishmen pissing on Camden's High Street that he had those urinals built at the intersection with Parkway, or at least that is what someone told Eileen once. Kilburn had no such literary benefactor. It was gritty and workaday, what Americans would call blue collar. In this part of London, you pissed in the streets, G. B. Shaw be damned. To be sure Kilburn was still Irish, but now it also was a kind of League of Nations. Veiled women from the Middle East passed by in black robes. Little children still wore silk jackets they probably brought with them from China. African children spoke with perfect working-class London accents, the kind of speech that pronounced words like computer and butter without the t's. But Kilburn was more chalk and cheese than a melting pot, more a collision of cultures than an harmonious merge.

Eileen was reminded of her own childhood in Dublin. She still remembered that her family's kitchen was in the basement—the lower ground floor—of the terraced house in which they lived. She loved that house, the classic urban dwelling, with its lower ground floor that led to the garden out back. Up the front steps, you walked to the elevated ground floor of the house, and above that were the bedrooms. The kitchen was large, much bigger than the one they would use in Sandymount when they finally moved away from central Dublin. Eileen remembered their dog, a big Irish terrier, and she remembered her aunts and cousins visiting them and standing in that big kitchen. It had French doors opening onto the garden.

Eileen's mother was not the world's worst cook. But her mother was not the best either. Her food was nutritional but not tasty. Her father, the good doctor, had the unfortunate habit of not charging his more indigent patients. He was an idealist by instinct and a man of medicine and science by necessity. He had a few dishes which he liked to make and which he made well: Welsh rarebit ("rabbit"); lamb stew; spaghetti Bolognese (spag-bol); and even the occasional curry dish (dal, saag paneer, etc.). They had food to eat, her mother liked to remind them, even if it was not as delicious or redolent as their neighbors' meals. That food smelled of garlic and herbs. The most herbaceous Eileen's family ever got was to use parsley with lamb, though never at the expense of mint jelly, and the parsley was usually only decorative.

An old neighbor who had worked as a barmaid in her day, one day in the laundry room of the Hotel Kilburn said to Eileen: "Kilburn is a tip!" But Kilburn was not a tip; it was more like a scrum. People moved in every direction banging into one another. Eileen had taken to circumventing the high street. If she needed to go to the post office, she would wait until she was in Hampstead—where the queues were shorter—or Camden Town—where the long "lines" went faster than Kilburn. (Of course, there were no 'lines' in any of these places, as no one called them that, but rather queues, only Eileen could not help but be reminded of her husband Santiago Santa who spoke of lines, not queues.) Eileen had picked up such expressions as "lines" from the long years she spent with him, as well as other niceties of his New York speech patterns and peculiarities. He wore *pants* instead of *trousers*, smoked *cigarettes* instead of *fags*, and stood in *lines* instead of *queues*. He stood in lines as a boy, he said, and he stood in lines as a man, too, and even when he was famous, he still stood in lines. It was the nature of America that a successful Black man still had to wait.

Instead of going to the grocery stores on the high street in Kilburn, Eileen took to going into the little shops on Abbey Road or walked down to Maida Vale or Little Venice sometimes, rather than approach Kilburn High Street with, not so much crowds, as throngs, hordes, or as a friend called anyone not himself, "you lot." Of course, you lot was really Eileen herself, the unwashed masses of Kilburn, "the bloody Irish," as she once heard it so lovingly put, in the days when terrorists were Irish instead of Middle Eastern. The former terrorists lived in County Kilburn, as Eileen also heard it called, with great humor and affection. Kilburn was like Dublin, Galway, or Limerick, crowded Irish places. They were not much different, for that matter, from parts of Brooklyn or Boston or Chicago.

But Kilburn *was* different.

On the surface, it possessed the Irish penchant for the shambolic, even the anarchic, like her family's own nightly dinner times, which were more like food fights than meals, and more like gun battles than supper. This organized chaos reminded Eileen of how the Irish prayed, never in unison, always to their own drummers, in their own biological rhythms. She had heard this joyful noise since childhood, no one saying the Hail Marys and Our Fathers together, but in a group, though always apart, at one's own rhythm and pace, one's inner musical cadence or the soul's beat, the heart's syncopation, the spirit within all of us. Later she would come to think of this discrete way of praying as deeply spiritual, each person finding a personal beat to communicate with God. Eileen did not mean to equate Kilburn High Street as being a spiritual experience; it had a way of robbing your energy, of sucking the life out of you. It had a way of wearing you down in the manner of the professional boxer who leans on his opponent in the later rounds, exhausting the opponent further, then setting him up for the kill.

If Eileen took the Number 31 bus from Camden Town, invariably she got off the stop before Kilburn High Street, and walked the street along Abbey Road—the long and winding road that led to Boundary Road and her flat. There were green grocers, corner grocers, and even a Middle Eastern super market, and yet sometimes she just had to go to Sainsbury's on the High Road for certain things, though never Marks and Spencer which seemed like the laziest way in the world to make dinner, not a food-lover's place but rather an emporium for someone overrun by the vagaries of the New Age, busy, busy, busy me, I'll simply pop this bag of veggies in the water to boil, and voila, a gourmet meal. Eileen wanted tomatoes, garlic, olive oil, parsley, lemon juice, pepper and salt added at her pace and taste, at her own leisure and doing.

This was a Sainsbury's day, much as she dreaded coming onto the High Street to shop. Eileen had run out of money after paying the weekly rent. But she remembered that—although all the other credit cards were frozen because she was at the limit with each—she had paid this one on time and there was enough credit available for a carefully selected week or so of groceries, and maybe even top up the mobile phone to make some calls, not just receive them. She might even be able to get another Zone 2 weekly travel card for the local tube and the buses. Whatever the outcome of this trip, she had no fear of embarrassment because she seemed to think that she knew no one in Kilburn. So Eileen went into Sainsbury's to shop, and who should she run into but Olga, from a job counseling group Eileen attended, at the strawberries, and in the dairy was a woman named Roberta, whom she knew from her teaching days at Surbiton University , and by the checkout she saw another person named Casey from Camden meetings. Thank God I have some credit, Eileen thought, and am able to buy some groceries, am able to feel civil and centered, alive and well. Thank God I was not whingeing about being broke and complaining that I had nothing to eat. People frankly were sick of hearing her sob story—or so she thought.

Each item that she placed in her hand-held blue plastic basket made the contraption buckle.

She had entered Sainsbury's around four o'clock of a halcyon summer day in late June, not too hot, one of those cloud-scudding blue skies that John Constable painted in Hampstead a few miles east, and a few hundred years ago. Even the bumping and abutting of Kilburn High Road had a rhythm to it, a musical shuttle like bebop or Thelonious Monk's thunkingly melodious piano.

Eileen started in produce, placing cheap, delicious strawberries in the blue basket. These were native ones, nearly at perfection, or maybe just past it, as the expiry date was that day, and she'd luckily found a pack that wasn't bruised or rotten. Next she picked a pack of blueberries from Spain, more expensive, she thought, but one of her extravagances. Didn't the doctors and nutritionists say that there was nothing healthier than blueberries? It was a superfood, whatever the hell that was. Eileen also got some curly parsley, cheaper than the flat kind, less tasty, too, but good in a fresh tomato sauce for pasta. She also got some new potatoes, a bunch of cherry tomatoes, two for the price of one. Then came carrots (organic) and apples and ginger for juicing through the week. She topped it off with some Fair Trade bananas.

In the dairy Eileen got three cartons of orange juice

for two pounds sterling and a big hunk of cheddar cheese for a little over two pounds. She bought a big tub of plain organic yogurt, wishing she could buy Rachel's vanilla yogurt, but she'd already indulged herself with the blueberries, and now she needed to move on. Lastly, before leaving the dairy section entirely, Eileen bought some grated Parmesan cheese from Reggiano, Italy, expensive, but the best tasting of this cheese, and her rationale was that it lasted a long time, which it did. Next she bought a big bag of brown organic rice and a big bag of penne pasta, but no sun-dried (sun-kissed, the jar says) tomatoes as she already had some at the flat. Eileen then got some dark rye flatbread crackers and a big, cheap bag of Scottish porridge oats for a month of breakfasts. She bought sweetened, organic soya milk, and some Sainsbury's instant coffee, and then got some Dove soap and deodorant, some toothpaste, and looked for cheap bread and some olive oil. Logically, the olive oil should have been with the pasta and the tomato sauces, but in this Sainsbury's, it was in the back of the store, with bread, condiments, and eggs.

The handle on the plastic basket was bowing, and so Eileen grasped the heavy load with both hands, cradling it in her arms as if it were a baby. In the way a child was precious, so were those groceries because Eileen didn't think she could afford them until she checked the various credit card statements from the month before, and then she saw this window of grace, and therefore went to the bread basket of Kilburn High Road to affect the transfer of credit for food. In the scheme of things, Eileen felt like a millionaire, like a million bucks, i.e., like five-hundred-and fifty-five-thousand pounds, give or take a shilling.

Eileen put down the bulging market basket, this horn of plenty, and she recalculated its expense, estimating it to be thirty pounds, well within her credit limit and budget, and then she re-examined the grocery list, making sure that there was nothing there that still needed purchasing.

In recent months Eileen had taken to going to the Tate Modern to look at four magnificent paintings by Cy Twombly called *Quattro stagioni*, the "Four Seasons." The Serpentine Gallery also had his drawings on display, and the Gagosian Gallery in King's Cross showed ten new paintings and a sculpture. In all of these shows and on all his paintings, Twombly wrote words in pencil, then scratched them out, and wrote other words. The seasonal paintings—the Vivaldian paintings—had poems and words from poets like Dante. The words in the drawings, as she recalled, were more muted, and the ten new paintings didn't always have words at all, except the occasional word Gaeta, and the date. Twombly, an American, had lived in Italy for nearly half a century, and Gaeta is where he had lived. Eileen thought of him because her grocery list had words that had been written over and crossed out, so that her own list resembled a palimpsest, the same way that Cy Twombly's paintings were. Her words were in blue ink, the lines through them in black, only because she had used the blue pen at the flat, and had the black pen in her pocket in the supermarket, a chance occurrence, a happenstance more than a willed artfulness like the paintings had come into being. It was less Cy Twombly than Kurt Schwitters, an art of poverty and circumstance rather than imagination and wealth.

In fact, the list bore no resemblance to art. It was a life list, as sustenance, a boon, a blessing, a gift. Eileen had imagined she would eat nothing but a crazy salad of air and anger, vinegar and despair for the next month. Instead she had a blue plastic market basket bursting at its seams with food and provender, with the abundance of life.

Here is the list Eileen used:

olive oil   bananas
oatmeal   blueberries
strawberries
brown rice

soya milk   cheese (Norwegian Jarlsberg)
o.j.   Parmesan cheese
penne pasta   instant coffee   deodorant
top up phone for 5 pounds

The list seemed modest enough, but Eileen had managed to improvise from it the way a jazz musician might take a popular musical standard and give it pure, spontaneous form. She had added strawberries, apples, carrots, and ginger, just like Charlie Rouse adding his saxophone solos to Thelonious Monk's piano music. Eileen had plucked fruit from the bins into the blue basket the way a bass player—Ahmed Abdul-Malik at the Five Spot Cafe in August 1958 with Monk—plucked improvisational chords on the big, stand-up bass, full of life's rhythms, really full of optimism in this sea of despair, not Kilburn High Road, but Eileen's own later life, so seemingly hopeless and foregone. Now she had been given a momentary stay against annihilation; she had been given a governor's stay against execution. She had enough credit to buy this motherlode of groceries.

Eileen smiled at the people in front of her and in back of her in the queue—the line, Santiago said—to check out. They looked at Eileen as if she were crazy. After all, this was not some arty redoubt like Hampstead; it was working-class Kilburn, tough and no-nonsense, a commonsensical place, practical, crowded, and blindingly efficient in how it gave people what they wanted, then shot them back out onto the High Street, bag-laden, poorer, but with the potential to be less hungry, perhaps even less grumpy, less angry and feeling alone. They would eat dinner with family, watch television, and go to bed with their stomachs full. Eileen saw nothing but hope on this check-out queue, this queue that was like a stairway to heaven, if she might sample from Led Zeppelin.

Then came her turn. The check-out person wore a badge that said her name was Mary. Eileen had encountered her many times. This Mary was decent enough, not harsh like the other clerks. There was a note of compassion in her face, especially her eyes. Like Eileen, Mary looked as though she lived by herself or perhaps with an elderly parent. At any rate, Mary had never married; that was obvious. She was a big, round, slovenly sort of woman, the kind you see everywhere in America, especially in the countryside. Eileen imagined that eating was probably her only pleasure. Yet Eileen was not a big, round, slovenly woman, but in every other way, she thought that she resembled that clerk Mary, who clearly was not American but Irish or working-class British.

The groceries zipped through Mary's scanner, and the end result was a figure just over thirty pounds, well within Eileen's credit limit. She would top off the mobile at the cigarette counter near the exit. Then she would go home to cook dinner, not watch television because she had none, but maybe listen to jazz on the radio, and actually go to bed with her belly full, no food anxiety, no mad jealousy of other people's good fortune, no desire to be anyone but who she was, Eileen Coole; she would be stuffed, sated, elated, sleepy, and ready to drift into the deepest slumber. Eileen fumbled with opening the last of the plastic bags, her hands all thumbs, and Mary and the person behind Eileen popped open the bags for her to fill the remaining items into them. Eileen then handed Mary her credit card, and waited for the check-out lady to come back with the slip for her to sign.

"I'm sorry," Mary said, "your card has been declined."

Eileen had bagged everything now, the olive oil, the juice, the instant coffee, the bag of penne, the fruits, the cheese, the yogurt, the oats, and all.

"Declined?" she asked.

"That's right," Mary said. "Declined."

Mary asked what Eileen wanted to do.

"I don't understand," Eileen said. "I checked my credit before going out, and it was fine."

"What's the problem?" the brusque assistant manager asked, stepping over to unclog the logjam Eileen had created in this queue.

The assistant manager was small and angular, brusque, bristly even, impatient to be done with Eileen or this problem or whatever it was. The assistant store manager had a touch of Irish in her voice, but not that lyrical Irish of Eileen's mother and grandmothers, nor any of the compassion of the clerk Mary. This was the clipped brogue of angry head sisters in parochial school. Mary explained to her manager that Eileen's card had been declined.

"Do you have another card?" the assistant manager asked.

Eileen had many cards. The only problem was that none of them worked. No, she said, that was the only card she had at the minute.

"Then there's nothing we can do," the assistant manager told her. "You can go off and call the credit card company to sort it out straight away and I'll hold your groceries at the courtesy counter in the front of the store for a half hour."

As Eileen walked back along the Kilburn High Road towards Maida Vale to the south, it seemed like every mother and child, every drunken father, every drunken bum and vagrant, bumped into her and shouted for her to watch where she was walking. Veiled women dressed from head to toe in black, with only a slit in the veil for their eyes, also bumped into her, and let fly with what Eileen imagined were infelicities of the Arabic or Farsi tongues. African women, who were taller than Eileen by a head, told her to watch her step, to look where she was going. Teenagers in blue nylon jackets and pants with white stripes down the sides of them shouted in her face, and their girlfriends with their loopy gold earrings called out things like "Yo, bitch" or "Watch out, ya feckin' eejit!" Eileen walked off crestfallen, a black cloud over her head like Pigpen in the Peanuts comic strip she read religiously when she lived in Iowa City. She walked along the High Road to a call shop and called up the credit card company to sort out what had happened. Though Eileen had paid the credit card bill with cash in a bank, she was told that it was not credited for four days—two days after the due date—and the late fee, plus interest, plus being fined for going over her credit limit—which they mistakenly put Eileen over—closed down her credit line automatically. They were sorry, the voice on the end of the telephone line said, but "there is nothing we can do about it, madame." So Eileen went back to her flat at the beginning of Maida Vale, stomach growling, arms empty of any provender, and she wondered how much longer she could continue to live like this.

SHELTERED

The laundry and community room were in the sheltered manager's office. It was a small flat on the second floor landing of the housing scheme in central London. The laundry room was in the kitchen, and the scheme manager's office was next to the community room. Sometimes people from the sheltered accommodation sat in the community room as they did their laundry, as it was a way for them to see neighbors, have a chat and catch up with them. Eileen's wash had finished and now she waited for the drying cycle to end, but it was taking longer than she expected, so she sat in the community room reading one of the many brochures from the council. This particular brochure was advising them not to let people into their flats without the person showing some kind of identification.

Betty Blue Blossom came into the common room and asked—

"Is the manager around?"

"I haven't seen her," Eileen said.

"She might be around," Betty said, "and you still mightn't have seen her."

Eileen knew better than to take the bait, so she hung fire and drilled her eyes into the brochures in her lap. Here was an interesting one about the police and how they patrolled the housing estates. She had been living at Hampstead Road for a while, having finally vacated the

Hotel Kilburn after the mugging in front of it, so she had already had a few encounters with Miss Blossom.

Joe McGardle sat in one of the community-room chairs, staring off into space.

"Us old folks should stick together, eh, Joe?" Betty Blue asked.

"I'm just here for the tea," Joe said.

"We go way back, eh, Joe?"

"I'm here for the tea, Miss Blossom."

"You can call me Betty."

"Miss Blossom," Joe said, "I'm not much for dialogue, especially between the sexes. Once I finish me tea, I'm back to me flat."

To prove his point, Joe took a slug of tea from his porcelain cup, one of the many oddly unmatched mugs and cups on the shelves in the kitchen. People were encouraged to come in, make themselves a cuppa, and have a bit of *craic* with the scheme manager or another neighbor.

Betty looked at Eileen.

There was probably twenty years difference in their ages, making Betty one of the oldest tenants in the building.

"Are you all right?" Eileen asked her.

"Do you want a polite answer?" Betty Blue Blossom asked.

"I want a truthful answer," Eileen said.

"I'm not well," Betty said.

"What is it?"

"Everything," Betty said.

"Where?"

"Everywhere."

When Eileen first moved to Hampstead Road, Betty gave her a bit of advice. She said: "If you want benefits, you don't want to go to the council on your best day. You go on your worst day, Eileen. You go to the council when you are feeling like being at death's doorstep. You go when you are like the walking dead. That's the day to go to the council for benefits—when you are beyond all repair." Then she beamed. "My benefits are nothing to sneeze at."

Betty had been a stripper and a bartender in Soho in her day. But her day was long ago, and she was an old dumpy lady now. She had seizures regularly, so she was supposed to be monitored, but sometimes she lay in a pool of saliva, blood, and urine for days before anyone bothered to knock on her door.

Eileen had once been more proprietary towards her, but Betty was not always the nicest person to deal with, and so Eileen tried to let go with love, not always the easiest thing to do with old people in one's own building.

The scheme's manager used to have regular tenant's meetings, but Betty would show up and start shouting at everyone, and nothing was accomplished, people getting up and leaving before the meeting ended. She liked to tell people about her late husband who was schizophrenic, but "the nicest chap you'd ever want to meet," Betty used to say, but sometimes it seemed as if maybe it was Betty who was the schizophrenic. She could be a turmoil of voices, finger pointing at everyone, paranoid to the point of making your skin crawl.

"That's a lot of malarkey," she once told Eileen, vis a vis nothing.

"What?" Eileen asked.

She had just gotten on the elevator and pushed the button for the second floor.

"Everything," Betty shouted.

"Be specific," Eileen said.

"The council," Betty told her.

"The council?"

"They're always in our business. Up our arses. In our affairs. Sucking the life out of us. Maggots. Motherfuckers."

The elevator stopped on 2, the doors opened, and Eileen stepped off.

"It's some nice weather we're having lately," Betty called out as the doors began to close and Eileen walked quickly down the outdoor landing to her flat.

Back in the common room, Joe said: "I'm scared."

"About what?" Betty Blue asked.

"Things," he said.

"Be specific. That's what Eileen says."

"The moon," he said.

"The moon?" Betty asked.

She laughed, though calling it a laugh was misleading; it was more of a cackle.

"Bloody hell, Joe, you ain't making a bit of fuckin' sense today."

"I'm here for the ice cream," Joe said.

"There ain't no ice cream today," Betty said. "That's for the summer party, once a year. We have a ways to go before they give us ice cream sandwiches to eat. It's already September, Joe, and the autumn leaves are falling, like the song says."

"I like the tea," Joe said.

"We all like the tea," Betty told him.

"There's no order here," Joe said.

"Order's given too much exposure," Betty shot back.

"No sense," Joe said, almost as if he were talking about the weather or a change in the season.

Eileen heard the dryer snap off, she stood, went into the kitchen to check her laundry. Everything was dry, and so she stuffed the clothes into a plastic Sainsbury's bag she used for her washing day. She waved goodbye to Betty and Joe, opened the door, and shot down the landing to her own flat, placed the key in her door, and settled into the confined quarters of her newest domain.

Hampstead Road's version of sheltered accommodation was at an improbable and noisy intersection near Euston Road, with the train station only a few blocks away. But Eileen was grateful to be gone from the Hotel Kilburn and its environs. If nothing else, she had this new flat to be thankful for.

Eileen adjusted to the noise and even the drug addicts outside her bedroom window and she settled in to her new flat.

She did not like the tea in the common room, so she

put on the electric kettle in her own kitchen and made herself a cuppa with her own tea bags and milk. With the big mug, she went into the room she called the studio, where she wrote and made little paintings and read her books and tried to block out the noise of traffic on Hampstead Road in the front rooms, which were the kitchen, bathroom and the hallway. Eileen had a balcony beyond the door in the studio, and when she felt more ambitious and hopeful, she grew tomatoes and herbs and sometimes managed to get an olive tree to blossom in the dreary light of central London.

There was no view out her studio window, as her flat faced another flat across Foundry Mews. In that facing flat, she had watched a small boy coming of age. One day he would become a teenager and, older still, leave his mother behind. His parents did not look British; they had an Eastern European look, all of them with dark hair, bushy eyebrows, and prominent noses. Everyone seemed to come from someplace else. On this tiny estate, there were Somalis and Russians, Serbs and Nigerians, but mostly there were people from Bangladesh, the dominant ethnic group in the neighborhood. No one was English or at least no one any longer admitted such an identity except in the context of sports—the Olympics, football, and rugby football, the Six Nations and all that rubbish. A lot of the Irish in the building said they were British, though, usually qualifying it by saying that they were London Irish.

Being British was a clever fiction. That is what most

of the Irish back home did not realize. There was really no such thing as a British person, although there was something called the British government. Being British was clever because it was like longitude and Greenwich Mean Time, something that was as much cultural and imperial as it was scientific. Eileen had no problem with such fictions; they were part of life in London. Being Irish was its own kind of clever fiction, though being Northern Irish was the cleverest fiction of all. When Eileen worked, the British government treated her as if she were one of their own, taking out their taxes and other assessments. But at the end of the day, she had less restrictions than a British citizen. She could come and go as an Irish citizen, especially as she also held an American passport from her marriage to Santiago Santa.

London was both lonely and liberating in equal measures.

Sitting in her studio and sipping her tea, Eileen stared out the window at the blank brick wall that faced her. She felt so much younger than the other people in this sheltered accommodation. Her only reason for being there was because she could not afford any other kind of housing and she qualified for it, being indigent and in her sixties and a drug addict in recovery. But her neighbors hummed "Always Look on the Bright Side of Life," while Eileen hummed a song like Joni Mitchell's one about the river, which Joni had recorded with Herbie Hancock. Eileen's memories were not about the Second World War, but of growing up in the Fifties and coming of age in the Sixties, of being a student, drinking booze and smoking dope, and then shooting heroin in the Maghreb. Ah, heroin, she thought, wistfully, but only for a moment before she snapped back into the reality of who she was and where she was and why she was there. It was the Promises: don't regret the past or wish to shut the door on it, but also don't romanticize that past as if it provided something better than what she had at that moment, which was peace of mind, acceptance of her circumstances, and the courage to change the things she could.

The upside was that she was in the center of London and could get anywhere in under ten minutes, either by walking or hopping on the public transportation, the bus or the Underground, which was free because she was now old enough to have a Freedom Pass. London might be a hard place to meet someone new, friend or lover, but you could do whatever you pleased, become whomever you wanted to be, and not be accountable to anyone.

After folding and putting away her laundry, Eileen went out for a walk. It was a rare autumn day that was not overcast or raining. She did not own fancy walking shoes or have a Barbour jacket. Her kit was modest, comfortable trainers, jeans, jumper, nylon jacket, cotton porkpie hat from Marks and Spencer, looking a bit like every other older woman out for an afternoon stroll in Regent's Park, except that her curly locks of red hair gave her a slightly clownish look when she wore the porkpie hat.

What made Eileen different was her long gait, her legs seeming to stretch twice as far as anyone else's step. Plus, being a loner, she did not walk in any way to accommodate others. Her stride was purposeful and accelerated, rapid and efficient. She did not saunter or tarry. She walked like an army marching into battle. Her pace was bullet-like, but as she ruminated, it slowed down, sometimes even coming to a halt on the Broadwalk, as she seemed to look at autumn colors on a tree, but really was lost in a movie that only she could see in her mind's eye. Her face was blank and pensive. But then again she was not out walking to have conversation with anyone; she walked to get exercise after being cooped up in her tiny flat for too many days because of the weather.

Her wild mop of red hair stood out on the sides of her porkpie hat like an Irish Afro. Redheads did not lose their hair color as quickly as others, so even in her sixties, Eileen was still a redhead, although it was now enhanced by bottles of stuff from Boots the pharmacist as well as the hairdressers—one step up from Mr. Toppers—on Tottenham Court Road.

"Do you have a pound or two?" a young woman asked her on the Broadwalk.

"No money, love."

"Just a quid."

"Nothing, darling."

"Don't be such a bitch."

"I'm skint," Eileen said.

This was not the first time this young woman had accosted her in Regent's Park. The woman had come up to her on Hampstead Road, too, and in the Euston Station.

Eileen had seen her in Tolmers Square, buying heroin when it used to be sold there openly by the drug gangs.

"You look all right."

"Looks are deceiving."

"Bloody hell," the young woman said, and stormed off.

At least it did not go any further than that, as sometimes it did. No one ever seemed to believe that Eileen was as broke as she really was. There was something about her that seemed, if not affluent, then a bit better off than the street people were. Which was true. She had a roof over her head. She ate simply and even well. Her needs were met, if not her wishes and desires. Perhaps wishes and desires were overrated. They only made one miserable, whereas having one's needs met was gratifying, a moment to be grateful for. Eileen noticed that people often mistook one's education for wealth, plus she had not grown up poor in Dublin.

Eileen looked at her watch and remembered that there was supposed to be a tenant's meeting at the manager's office of the sheltered accommodation where she lived and so she quickly walked back towards the eastern edge of the park, exiting onto Albany Street and then turned left onto Drummond Street and walked back to her flat at 40 Hampstead Road.

The tenant's meeting was already in full swing when she walked into the manager's office and into the community room where several of the tenants were sat listening to the council's head of sheltered housing, a little ginger-haired man named Connor Dougherty. As Eileen took a seat, she heard Connor say: "In order to provide you with better quality service, we've cut back the manager's hours from five days a week to two mornings."

"How is that more quality?" one of the oldest tenants, Giles Foster, asked.

"We'll give you more attention than now," Connor Dougherty said straight-faced and without blinking.

"We don't get any attention now," Betty Blue Blossom shouted, almost at the top of her lungs, which was considerable.

"I'm not about to get into a shouting match with you, Miss Blossom."

"I haven't raised me voice."

"You don't have permission to abuse the staff with your shouting."

"I've been most civil, Mr. Dougherty."

Connor Dougherty looked sternly at Betty. He had the face of an altar boy, but the personality of a drill sergeant, although he was not a very big person and his manners were not particularly masculine, which made him less a drill sergeant than a mother superior at a wayward school for delinquent girls.

"I must warn you and the others, Miss Blossom, that I have the power to terminate your lease at any time."

Dickie Farrell, one of Eileen's nearby neighbors, called out: "You're talking bollocks."

"Very well, I'll leave then."

"You haven't addressed our concerns," Betty shouted.

Mr. Dougherty pointed his index finger at Betty Blue Blossom.

"You have no right to verbally abuse me."

"It was you who called this bloody meeting," Dickie Farrell said.

"I'll have you sectioned, Mr. Farrell."

"For asking a question?"

"For insubordination, sir. You have no right to abuse council staff. There are people dying to get into these flats."

"There are people dying in these flats who live here, love," Betty called out.

She nodded her head affirmatively towards Eileen, as if to form a wall of solidarity against the council staff.

"We're just here to get information," Eileen said.

"Who are you?" Connor Dougherty asked.

"I'm Eileen Coole," she said.

"They'll give you a bloody feckin' brochure, Eileen, and then tell you to shut the feck up."

"I'll give her nothing of the kind, Miss Blossom," Connor shouted back at Betty.

Betty muttered something under her breath, but Eileen did not hear what she said.

"What did you call me?" Connor said, the outrage rising up in him. "I will not be made a figure of fun."

"You heard me," Betty said.

"Silence!" Connor shouted.

The room got quiet.

"I won't be silenced," Betty said. "You can't shut me up."

"I'll call the police," Connor said.

"Go ahead, call them."

One of the old men from the corner called out: "Betty's going to have a seizure. Stop shouting at her."

Betty then fell to the floor, from a seizure, until she became unconscious.

There was just a moment of silence before anyone moved to help her.

"Let that be a lesson," Connor said.

He grabbed his jacket from the back of a chair and started to head for the exit.

"What's the lesson?" Dickie Farrell asked as some of the others worked on Betty on the floor.

Eileen sat in her chair, looking at Betty, then looking up at Connor Dougherty at the door.

"Let this remind you what happens when you thwart me and the council. Let it be a reminder."

"Call an ambulance!" someone shouted.

"He killed her."

"She'll come around," Connor said.

After Connor Dougherty left and the ambulance attendants arrived, a few people from the sheltered housing remained behind in the room after Betty Blossom was carted off on a gurney.

"Someone should make a documentary of our lives?" an old woman named Maria from the first floor said. She was from Goa in the Indian Ocean. She moved quite slowly whenever Eileen saw her outside, even though the woman was younger than Eileen. She was one of the three Marias in the building. The other two were Spanish and Portuguese.

"Who would watch it?" the Spanish Maria asked.

"We would," the Portuguese Maria said.

Spanish Maria said that "we already know about our lives. We're living them."

"Someone should know," Portuguese Maria declared.

"Tell the council," Goa Maria said.

Everyone laughed. Goa Maria was a comedienne.

"I'm losing all patience," Spanish Maria said.

Goa Maria said that she hadn't had any patience for years.

"Hope is overrated. And so is patience. Especially when you are old. Personally I would rather have a handsome young man than hope."

"It's hopeless," Spanish Maria said.

"It could be worse," Goa Maria answered.

This was all spoken, the three Marias' conversation, in a spirited, hopeful way. It wasn't like Joe McGardle's hopelessness or even Eileen's own hopeless moments that seemed to freeze in place, usually in her flat, not going out for days.

Everyone cleaned up the cups and saucers, the plates of cookies, and the empty milk cartons and threw away the rubbish and washed up the dishes and went back to their flats in the sheltered accommodation.

As Eileen walked towards her flat on the landing, she heard the three Marias as they waited for the elevator to come.

"Thyme," Spanish Maria said.

"It's just gone three o'clock," Portuguese Maria answered.

"No, thyme, the seasoning."

"Two past the hour," said Portuguese Maria.

Goa Maria spelled it out for her: "T-H-Y-M-E."

Portuguese Maria said: "You're W-E-L-C-O-M-E."

NO JUSTICE / NO PEACE

After they married, Eileen traveled all around the world with Santiago for two years. They often went on trips within trips, visiting Patagonia, for instance, while he performed in Buenos Aires. They stayed and sometimes lived in hotels, motels, B & B's, guest houses, even private apartments. In London, they stayed at the White House apartments, near Regent's Park, where a lot of musicians lived. More often than not, Santiago Santa was the lead-off act for some prominent jazz musician, though more and more he was becoming the featured attraction. Back in the world, as America was called, they stayed at his place in Oakland or, sometimes in New York, visiting his daughter who lived out in Brooklyn. He had a friend who let him use his three-room tenement flat on East 10th Street near Second Avenue, and Eileen mentioned that she probably lost her virginity in that same building four years earlier on her way to Iowa, and several years before she wound up in Berkeley. His name was Stan Swanberger, a young poet; she had met him at a party on the Lower East Side. It was her birthday. Stan "deflowered" her after the party; that is how Eileen described it. She had smoked pot for the first time, and the next thing she remembered, they were naked on the mattress in the living room, fucking their brains out.

"I used to live in that building," Santiago said. "I wish I was there when you decided to lose your cherry. I could have helped you out."

"Go on now," Eileen said, laughing.

"No, really," he said, sounding very Brooklyn.

When Santiago was in New York, but not performing, he often sounded very Brooklyn. Little words and phrases: he would mispronounce the words "pause" and "paws." He said the word "huge" as if it were spelled "yuge." When people asked him how he was doing, he answered by saying: "How you doin'?"

They would be out walking around the city, something they did almost every day they were there, even on days when he had to rehearse or it was snowing. They went to museums and galleries in the day time, saw art movies on rainy afternoons, and in the evening went to off-Broadway plays or spent the evening in some club where a friend of his might be playing. They ate out almost every evening: Polish restaurants on Avenue A, Chinese places further down the Bowery in Chinatown, Japanese restaurants in Midtown Manhattan or they would go to the Upper West Side and dine in a cheap but delicious Greek restaurant that was popular with poets at that time. Her favorite West Side restaurants were Cuban Chinese, and sometimes they hopped the subway and got off at 79th and Broadway, eating at La Caridad, the Cuban Chinese place a block south of the train station. Eileen went to a lot of poetry readings, and sometimes Santiago came along with her, but he was often too busy to go to a reading, as much as he wanted to accompany her to one. He performed, recorded, did radio shows, was even on television once in a while. He performed in a series at the New School and another series at the Museum of Modern Art. He sat in on gigs at the Five Spot or the Village Vanguard, the Village Gate or even at Slugs on 4th Street in the East Village.

Often they met up at Kennedy Airport, catching up on the plane to Europe or South America or the Far East.

They were proper bohemians, clean cut and neat and, in those days at least, didn't use too many drugs or drink too much, though Eileen let loose once in a while on one of her booze binges when she took no prisoners.

"I'm no fucking saint, Santa," she said.

"Well, I am," he answered. "That's how come they call me Santa."

Santiago Santa was of the Sixties, but the Sixties were gone like the flash of a blue flame on a match's tip. Murders (King, X, the Kennedys), betrayals (everywhere), suicides (Lenny Bruce by drug OD or the Buddhist monks going up in flames in Saigon); and then Richard Nixon (evil personified). Oakland was not the place it once was, Santiago said, not the place he chose to live in for so many years. There was even less justice, it seemed, less chance for people to excel and shine. He had been discussing with his wife Eileen where they might go. She already knew that the police and the FBI were formulating a case against him, not for any crimes committed, but because of who he was. In the 1960s, his music was described as angry, which to some extend it was. But he still composed his lyrical ballads, including "Eileen's Dream" and his most haunting ballad "Cathleen nee Houlihan."

His composition "Eileen, Good Night" was said to hark back to the blues of Leadbelly and take the listener up to "What's Goin' On" by Marvin Gaye. But the Sixties was also the era in which Santiago wrote, then performed over and over again, his classic post-bop jazz masterpiece "No Justice / No Peace."

There were two things that happened after the Sixties ended that made him want to leave the country. Four students were murdered by the National Guard at Kent State and a week later, there was the slaughter of students at Jackson State. Kent State happened on May 4, 1970; Jackson State's criminal assault on the students took place on May 15th. Jackson State's crimes occurred shortly after midnight. The police opened fire on peaceful, unarmed student demonstrators. Twelve people were injured. Two died.

"I cannot get their names out of my head," Santiago told Eileen. "Phillip Lafayette Gibbs and James Earl Green. Phillip Lafayette Gibbs and James Earl Green. Gibbs and Green. Phillip and James."

The Oakland police were about to say that Santiago Santa was involved in a Black Panther murder in Oakland. It didn't seem to matter that he had been in Japan at the time of the murder. This was post-Manson America. The established order didn't need facts, only drifts and their hunches, their political nuances, coupled with their fear and ignorance, the two horsemen of American prejudice. People believed a lot of crazy shit. Their beliefs superseded the facts. That's how Richard Nixon, as crooked as a crime lord, came into power, and how he escalated the Vietnam War, Santiago said, in order to end it. "How's that for an oxymoron?" Santiago asked. The Nixonian paradox: bring peace by killing all the motherfuckers on the planet. If you were inclined a certain paranoid white person way, you could say that Santiago Santa didn't have to pull any trigger. He gave the order; he was the kingpin. It did not matter that he was not a Black Panther himself; he did not stop talking about the Panthers whenever he performed. He was guilty by association, as prosecutors say of associates of crime lords or even the crime lords themselves. That was what the FBI was going to say. Although it had not been put into law yet, RICO laws were being formulated in order to arrest organized crime figures, and the police and the government saw the Black Panthers not so much as a political party than as a crime organization.

Eileen had known a fellow she went to University College Dublin with, and now he was a cell of the newly constituted Irish Republican Army (IRA) with their underground headquarters in San Francisco. This old friend—his name was Owen Rattigan—owned one of those twee Irish shops, down on Market Street, selling thick white Aran sweaters, saint-themed greeting cards, statues of Mary and Jesus, and even green plastic hats for St. Paddy's Day. He also sold rosaries and Bibles and Claddagh rings and medals of saints. Out of the back of the shop he provided, as another kind of service, which was less minty than his front of shop, Armalite rifles to the

Black Panthers. His cousin, an FBI agent, had told him that there was going to be a sweep of the various Panthers, but that they also planned to make a show arrest of Santiago Santa, to drive home a point. With regard to Santiago Santa, there was free speech and your First Amendment rights, unless you happened to be a handsome, black, charismatic jazz musician. Then all bets were off. He had become too vocal in his support of the Panthers, talking about them, not only at his concerts and shows in clubs, but also on the radio, and not just jazz stations. He would get on the airwaves anywhere that anybody would have him. That's why the FBI was going to nail his ass to a pole. At least Owen Rattigan, Eileen's old UCD friend, told her that was the reason for the putative arrest.

The order to arrest Santiago came from the top.

Richard Nixon, in his own inimitable way, alluded to Santiago's musical composition in a speech in Riverside, California months earlier: "There are no words in this composition, but it is a rallying cry for the disenfranchised to burn down our suburbs, rape our daughters, and install a radical socialist apparatus upon the American people— us, we the people—the silent majority. I, for one, will not tolerate this seizure of our Constitutional rights by the radical left, whether it be Santiago Santa playing his angry piano or some Black Power revolutionary toting an assault weapon as he enters a federal courthouse in Oakland, California. As Winston Churchill said: 'We shall fight them on the beaches, we shall fight them in the fields and in the streets.' We will fight the Santiago

Santas of the world wherever they are, composing music that incites rioting or black poets inciting riots in Newark with their poems. The Silent Majority is ready for them."

Santiago said: "The next thing that cracker asshole will be saying is that Miles Davis is inciting rioters with the music from *Kind of Blue*."

Eileen laughed.

"Now you're talking serious blather."

Yet there was some half-truth in what Nixon said in Riverside, California. People were inspired by Santiago's music, especially his composition "No Justice / No Peace." And what they were inspired to do was to revolt, to have an uprising, to uproot the status quo, which was Nixon and the FBI nationally, and the Oakland police locally. "No Justice" was an anthem and a battle cry, a call to arms, even if the arms were only akimbo, as they danced in protest to the status quo.

The FBI and Nixon and the Oakland police could not stop the music, only disrupt it momentarily. "No Justice / No Peace" had become a rallying cry for young black and white radicals, and they weren't about to stop listening to it just because Richard Nixon claimed that its lack of words was a clarion call to arms for the disaffected and the outlanders, the disgruntled workers and the students shouting for a revolution.

There did not have to be words to Santiago's song; the noise, the rhythms, the cadences said it all. His pounding on the piano keys. The snarling honk of the saxophone; the drummer out of control almost, slamming the skins with his sticks. The bass was not the stand-up kind, but the rock bassist kind, the beat deep inside you, thumping like a second heart.

"What are we going to do?" Eileen asked.

"We're getting the fuck out of here," Santiago said.

"Where?"

"The walls have ears," he said. Then: "Are you game?"

"Game," Eileen whispered.

He knew from the moment that he had met her that she was the one.

Santiago whispered to her that they were going to travel Indian style. She asked what that was. He held out his hand. "Whatever you can fit into the palm of your hand. We travel light. It's a metaphor, darling. You love metaphors. We each get a small suitcase. Seven pairs of socks, seven pairs of underwear. A sweater. A jacket. The clothes we're wearing. Cash in our pockets. Passports. I've already sublet the apartment in Oakland. We're leaving this morning."

"Today?"

"Yes, today," he said.

"For fuck's sake," Eileen whispered, almost saying it like a prayer.

He loved her foul mouth and her beautiful Irish face and her wild red hair. He loved her style, her tallness and thinness and the way she used words. But he especially was in love with her spirit; they were two souls that understood each other, sometimes without even saying a word. A nod or a smile was all that was needed to create the understanding.

Eileen and Santiago got into his antique Jeep station wagon and drove southward out of Oakland. By that evening they were past Los Angeles and heading towards the border. They drove until San Diego, staying the night on Coronado Island. In the morning, they got back into the old Jeep station wagon and drove into Ciudad Tijuana, where they spent another night, figuring out their plans, their strategies. This was something they had discussed since they had first met two years earlier. In their travels around the world, to France and Italy and Switzerland for festivals and concerts, to Tokyo and Osaka, Seoul and Pusan, and all the dusty small crowded music venues throughout Asia and the Far East, they had talked about there coming a time when they needed this plan to escape from the U.S., go into Mexico, then head to Cuba, which is what they were doing now.

They ditched the Jeep station wagon in Mexico City.

"I was going to get a new one soon anyhow," he laughed.

He sold the car for a surprisingly good price and he changed the pesos into traveler's cheques.

Within the week, they were in Havana, his second time there. Fidel was a big fan of Santiago's and had invited him to stay in Cuba. They lodged in a downtown Havana hotel while they sorted out what they were going to do, and Santiago, as he often did wherever they traveled, played regularly in the hotel's club.

The Cubans were aware of Santa's double life as a musician and a political activist; they liked him on both accounts. As a result they left him alone for the time being, not putting any demands on his presence in Havana. Then one day someone close to Fidel told Santiago about Algeria. The Cuban official—his name was Juan de la Cruz—said that Algiers was *"muy bueno"* and *"mas agradable."* So it was decided. The Santas would go to Algeria, for an open-ended stay. Algeria had shed its French colonial past a decade earlier. The Santas were informed that they were going to be taken to Algiers on a Cuban military transport plane. Their fellow passengers were a group of Cuban doctors being ferried to Algeria to offer their services and, then, as they told the Santas, to go down in western and central Africa, to deal with malaria and other medical problems in the region. In the Third World, Cuban medical doctors were highly esteemed , well trained and effective, the best from anywhere.

It was autumn, but you would not know it by the blue skies, the white houses, the palm trees everywhere in the city of Algiers. Unlike Nice, which they knew, Algiers did not have colorful houses, only these white ones, bare and defiant against the sunlight, which was the dominant quality of the city, its light. But downtown, Algiers did resemble places you might see in Nice's interior, away from the Promenade des Anglais, the working neighborhoods where Algerians lived. So in some ways it was Nice, only without the *joie de vivre*. Algiers was Mediterranean, but it was not a city in which people indulged their sense of *dolce far' niente*, the Italian thing about taking life lightly and enjoying oneself. No one took life lightly in Algiers.

No one seemed to be enjoying life, despite the fact that they had been free from France for the past ten years. The post-colonial world was one of struggle and survival, only a struggle that was free of the French yoke around their necks. Being free was not only a weight being lifted off the body politic and the immediate world, it also imposed a different kind of weight; was this the responsibility of surviving in a hostile world that had no intention of helping you to survive. Luckily, Algeria had incredible natural resources, including oil and gas, and a vast reservoir of minerals under the desert sand of the Sahara.

Back in Algiers, the day was hot and dry, the wind not coming off the Mediterranean Sea but out of the desert to their south, the Great Sahara, and its mysterious winds that gave some people inspiration and others bad headaches, pounding migraines, upset stomachs, and restlessness.

Eileen had the headaches. Santiago felt inspired.

He was not going to let the FBI, the CIA, and their COINTELPRO program destroy him or other musicians and poets affected by the government's interference in their lives.

"Fuck them," he said. "Fuck them where they breathe."

"Amen," Eileen said. "Can I get a witness?"

He laughed.

Santiago did not smile often, but when he did, his smile was electrifying, Eileen thought, and he was simply the most handsome man she had ever seen. At least that is what she still told herself. She was still on a pink cloud about meeting and then marrying Santiago.

Neither of them expected to be in Algeria for very long.

When things cooled down in America, perhaps they would go back to Oakland or, if the heat was still on there, live in New York or maybe set up shop in London. The people at Ronnie Scott's club in Soho were often asking him to come do a gig.

After a while Eileen asked: "Where the fuck are we?"

Her wild mop of red hair, unique wherever she went, made her stand out even more in Algiers. Her husband, on the other hand, looked the part, and fit right into life in post-colonial Algeria. Santiago kept a copy of Frantz Fanon's *Wretched of the Earth* on the nightstand next to their bed. His copy was in the original French, and sometimes he would read passages aloud to Eileen. He would read a few pages every night before going to bed.

"If only I could have met him," he said. "It is one of my regrets."

Though he was from the Caribbean, Fanon, a psychiatrist, had lived in Algeria and was deeply involved in its liberation. Alas, he had died ten years earlier, around the time of his book's publication.

"All the Panthers read his work," he said. "It was required reading."

"He was fucking brilliant," Eileen said. "*Wretched of the Earth* is a map for revolution."

A decade before the Santas came to Algiers, the revolution had defeated the French, and all the Europeans had been thrown out. Except for some red-haired, green-eyed Berbers in the mountains, Eileen Coole was not the kind of person you saw on the streets of Algiers in 1970. People stared at this odd Irish woman and the handsome man, her husband, whom everyone presumed was Algerian.

With regard to where they were, Santiago told her: "We're in the Maghreb. Algiers."

"I know where we are geographically," she said. "What baffles me is how we wound up here."

"The fuck should I know," he said, going Brooklyn on her. "All I know is that we are here."

Santiago understood what Eileen was feeling, as her presence was exceptional for the Algerians. If the Europeans had all been cast out, why was this clearly European woman still in their midst?

In those first months when they roamed around the city, people gathered around Eileen wherever they went. They touched her arms, so pale, her hair they touched, so red, they said, and sometimes she punched someone if they got too touchy-feely with her.

"Fuck off," she said, then calmed down when she realized it was a young girl or boy fascinated by her features.

"Haven't youse ever seen red hair before?" she asked, and Santiago explained that they did not know a word of English and that probably it was not a good idea to speak French to them. He began to pick up Arabic almost immediately.

It became clear in those first couple of months that in order to survive in this country, they would need to make some adjustments. What they had going for them—what Santiago had going for him—was that Algeria had no extradition treaties with the United States. But in order to live in Algiers, they needed a private space outside the city center, so they went looking for accommodation in the hills overlooking the sea and near the university.

They found a newly built modern one-story house with a great patio overlooking the Mediterranean Sea.

Without a manager now, Santiago let Eileen take on that duty. She booked his first gig in a football (soccer) stadium outside of Tangier in next door Morocco. From that first concert, Tangier became the place where they went to relax and escape from the tensions in Algeria. In Tangier, they used drugs, at first hash, but as time wore on, heroin. Revolutionary Algeria would punish you severely for using drugs.

Santiago shot up Eileen for the first time in a hotel in Tangier.

They would return to that hotel regularly.

Eileen and Santiago thought that they would stay in Algiers for a month, maybe two. Their French became impeccable, and his Arabic was passably good. "*La ilah illa'llah wa Muhammad rasul Allah*," Santiago often said. "There is no god but God, and Muhammad is the Messenger of God." It's true, the Algerians would say. *C'est vrai.* They settled in. Santiago now performed in two types of places—in emerging African countries and, abroad in Europe, behind the so-called Iron Curtain, in

Yugoslavia, the Ukraine, and Moscow. They traveled this way throughout the 1970s and even the next decade, at least, until the so-called Iron Curtain began to show rust and fell down one afternoon in Berlin. The only criteria for him to perform in a country was that there was no extradition treaty with the United States. Thus they found themselves in Pula at the southern tip of the Istrian peninsula, in the northwest corner of Yugoslavia. He performed in the Amphitheatre—a two-thousand-year-old Roman structure—and they stayed in a hotel steps away from where James Joyce had lived when he first went into exile in 1904.

Joyce had been a language teacher for Berlitz in Pula, and he managed to last six or seven months before pulling up stakes and going north into Trieste, where he stayed fifteen years, writing most of his major works.

"Bloody hell," Eileen declared, looking out the window of their hotel room in Pula and seeing the Arch of the Sergii, two-thousand-years-old and looking as fresh as ever.

Eileen's head was filled with Nora and James Joyce walking these streets, strolling under the Arch, taking their coffee at one of the nearby cafes. Like her, they were young and in love and Irish but really citizens of the world, Europeans, Joyce called them, and Eileen said to herself, European, yes, but also Mediterranean, as they now had settled into Algiers as their base whenever they went off on these whirlwind tours to play jazz to Santiago's acolytes.

"Alas," he said while they were in Pula, "we leave for Algiers tomorrow, so no more coffees under the canopy of trees on the Giardini, no more walks down to the sea to feed the seagulls bread. We are back to the salt mines of Algeria."

It was all said with a smile, wistful and pleased.

They walked, holding hands and still in love, down to the sea one last time. A ship, a gigantic container ship, was in drydock being serviced. When they looked up, Eileen grabbed Santiago's arm and said, "Look at the name of that drydocked ship, Santa."

He looked.

"Holy shit," he said, betraying his degrees from Columbia University and Julliard.

Its name was Santiago.

They walked back to the hotel, stopping at one of those outdoor cafes under the giant plain trees on the Giardini. As in Algiers, people stared at them, a well-dressed, tall, handsome Black man, and an extremely tall, thin, big-nosed, red-headed Irish woman, equally well dressed. Who were they? And more important, what were they doing in that part of Yugoslavia known as Croatia?

Ten years earlier, it was 1973, the Vietnam War winding down, but the Santas still lived in their self-imposed exile from the United States, guests of the revolutionary Islamic government of Algeria. The country was now fully independent of, not only France, but also Europe. Instead of looking north to the Mediterranean countries, it now faced south, into Africa, and its newly emerging countries. When it did not face south towards Ghana and the other African dynamos, Algeria turned westward towards Morocco and eastward towards Tunisia, Libya, and Egypt. Eileen ran nine miles every morning. She wore a blue nylon jacket and trousers, and a knitted skull cap she pulled down over her ears. She wore yellow Nike running shoes and had on white socks, part cotton, part synthetic. She went out in the dead of night, about four in the morning. She wore runner's gloves, just to keep her hands warm. It was cold at this time of night, in the early morning of the desert. In the hills, where they lived, at the intersection of sea and desert, it became cold after dark. The hills were where she ran. She ran up in the hills for about an hour and a half, sometimes two hours, every day, and she stretched for fifteen minutes at the start and finish of every run.

The Europeans were gone from Algiers, not a trace of them to be found, except for their architecture, which made the city still appear like a provincial French city.

Eileen knew right away that her distinct look might bring adverse attention.

She was too tall, too thin, too redheaded. She was unkempt, anarchic, a bit too bolshie for the Maghreb, even in revolutionary Algeria. Eileen Coole was not someone that Algerians were used to seeing, even when the French were there, and her oddness was not something new, as the Santas had been in Algeria for some time.

Once, in their first months in country, Eileen went

out for a run during the daylight hours. It was still early morning, but already suffused with desert heat. The light and the heat were more than just a slap in the face; it was a rude awakening. She had gone out running in shorts and a tee shirt, braless, and independent. That was something which no women did in Algiers. Then she had taken a wrong turn, and instead of coming back to the neighborhood where they now lived, she came into a more crowded warren closer to the downtown area, though still residential, not commercial.

Suddenly Eileen was surrounded on all sides by soldiers, their rifles pointing at her. She was handcuffed, arrested, thrown into a paddy wagon, and then charged with lewdness and indecency. Santiago figured out that something was wrong when she did not return at her usual time back to the house. She had been gone too long.

He made some telephone calls.

Someone called the police.

She was there, he was told, at the central police station downtown.

The soldiers had given her over to the police and the police had locked her up. They either spoke no French or refused to engage her in their arch enemy's language. Eileen had yet to learn any Arabic beyond a few simple phrases.

Santiago drove downtown in one of his sportscars. It was a Morgan, something that the Algerians had not seen before either. The steering wheel was on the right side, not the left. He walked into the police station wearing a sheer black almost see-through tee shirt, very French gangster. He also wore a yellow linen suit; only Santiago could pull off a yellow linen suit. On his feet: local sandals. He was very smartly North African looking, and they'd only been there just shy of a year. Unlike Eileen, who stood out, Santiago was very much a part of. He fit in seamlessly. His outfit was a kind of camouflage, making him almost invisible until he stood a few feet away from the policemen in the station.

They did not, the police, know who he was, but they knew, as the Irish say, that he was somebody. He had an air, a manner, a way about him, and how he moved. His rhythm was part of the sky and the sunlight and the sea and the desert. Perhaps he was a famous footballer (a soccer player) on the national team. He wore expensive dark sunglasses. He looked both very important and very street. He had a look that suggested that it was better to be his friend than his enemy, his brother rather than his brother's keeper.

His Arabic was good enough too.

For Eileen, he had brought along her nylon jacket and trousers, the synthetic skull cap she would wear in the early morning runs from that point onwards. By the end of it, Eileen sat sweating in the workout gear while Santiago spoke to the police in a patois of Arabic and French, offering them cigarettes, posing for a photograph with policemen and soldiers who had remained behind at the police station.

Eileen sat in a corner, fuming and ignored, muttering to herself under her breath.

All the charges were dropped.

In the Morgan, driving back into the hills near the university, she let Santiago know that she was not happy with her circumstances.

"I am not chattel," she kept saying, over and over, banging her fist into the dashboard. Then she shouted: "I'm not *fucking* chattel."

"No, you are not," he said, trying to soothe her, but it seemed to have the opposite effect.

He parked the Morgan in the driveway next to the stone patio. There were several other cars there, too, all Santiago's; he had a thing about cars.

Eileen was out of the Morgan before Santiago cut the engine. She didn't bother to open the door, but catapulted over the side of the car door and stormed off into the house.

A few days later, calmer, Eileen said, "I'm going to run in the night, when no one's around—like the boxers do."

"Boxers?" he asked.

"You know."

"No, I don't know, Eileen."

"I'm going to run around four in the morning when the fighters do their roadwork. Instead of running, I'm going to do roadwork."

"Oh," he said. Then he paused and asked. "How many cigarettes are you smoking?"

"It's a new habit," she said.

"I know it's new," Santiago said, "but just how many are you smoking, girl?"

Calling her "girl," which he often did, was both Black and Irish, and it usually made her laugh. The Irish called someone a girl no matter what their age, and the Black culture, at least in America, called people girl as a form of solidarity, and no matter how old or womanly the person was.

Eileen thought, counting up the daily round of fags in her mind.

"Eighty," she said, matter of factly.

"Eighty!?"

He was flabbergasted.

"Give or take a few one way or the other."

"That's four packs a day," he informed her.

"Well, how many *fucking* packs do youse smoke?"

"One," he said, "at most, usually when I'm working or composing or doing something."

"One?"

"Now, being here, chilling out, the police and the FBI off my case, I smoke five or ten cigarettes at most."

"We both smoke something less than a hundred," Eileen said.

"No, I smoke five or ten. You smoke eighty cigarettes. That's ten or fifteen times more than I smoke."

"I didn't smoke before we came to this hellhole on earth where women are nothing but chattel. I'm your personal possession. *Chattel personal.*"

"And how many miles are you running every day?"

"I don't see the connection, Santa."

She called him Santa when she was pissed off, and she was.

"You're running nine miles every day, and on top of that, you're smoking eighty cigarettes."

"I don't see what this has to do with you, man."

"You're my wife," he said. "We live together. I love you. I don't want to see you die. You're going to burst your heart, and then you're going to break mine. I am not going to meet another person quite like you, Eileen Coole, Cathleen nee Houlihan, daughter of Cuchulain, Red Branch king."

There.

It was out.

He smiled.

When Santa smiled, he showed the dimples in his cheeks.

He was irresistible, or so Eileen had once said.

When he smiled, he made perfect sense.

At the time, he was living cleanly, not smoking too much, not drinking, not using any drugs except when they went on holiday to Tangier. He ate well; he worked out in a tiny gym, next to his recording studio, at the back of the house.

"Listen," he said, "I know that being here is no picnic for you. But think of the options. I'm facing serious time back in the States. They'll convict my ass on some made-up charges, and then I'm going to be spending the rest of my life in one of Uncle Sam's prisons with a lot of other Black folk who are also innocent."

Algiers was edgy and a little paranoid, poor and wanting. It was not a holiday destination in those days.

In their home in the hills up by the university, Santiago regularly read Camus, but by the 1970s, the French and the Algerians had dismissed Camus as being just another *pied noir*, the Algerians who were of European background.

Now that Santiago's base was Algiers, he often thought of the writer. How could he not? Camus had grown up poor, even destitute, in the nearby city of Oran, a quieter version of Algiers. The French writer had become controversial towards the end of his life. People thought he was on the wrong side of the Algerian issue—on the wrong side of the revolution and the wrong side of history. In France, some intellectuals who wrote about jazz considered Santiago Santa another version of the *pied noir*, not really someone who was committed to Algeria the way that Frantz Fanon had been. Santiago had to laugh. He spend nearly all of his waking hours pursuing music and other issues, both with the same theme, which could be summed up simply as social justice.

"There can be no spirituality," Santa would say, "until there is social justice."

"*D'accord!*" Eileen said, sitting in a café with him when they still did such things in Algiers.

"Do what you love to do," Santiago said, "because jazz, like the arc of justice, is long, but life, man, life is short, and a real motherfucker."

They drank; Santa took drugs.

Life went on, motherfucker or not.

They were alone in Algiers, although they eventually managed to put together a sort of life. Now they embraced that other Joycean attribute—exile. They lived in the hills, not far from Eldridge's Embassy. They had a lovely white house, one story tall, modern and bare, with picture windows looking out upon the blue-green Mediterranean below.

There was a grand terrace, a table at which they sat, she writing words, he writing music. They ate lunch and sometimes dinner out there. When people visited, they would sit out on this terrace for hours, commenting on the beauty of the sea and sky, the elemental whiteness of the buildings, the heat and wind off the Sahara, and the whispered cadences of the Arabic that was spoken all around them.

Eileen stopped writing poetry or only wrote it rarely. What she did was to write regularly in a journal. She found a shop in downtown Algiers that sold stationary. There she regularly bought clairefontaine notebooks, keeping a journal daily for almost all of their years in Algeria. She even found an old Mont Blanc fountain pen in the display case of the stationer's, a pen that had sat in the case since a time before the French left the country. They sold it to her cheaply; she was a good customer, and they also threw in a bottle of blue ink. She never lost the habit of writing. What changed were the old forms, which had been abandoned; prose replaced poetry.

They would get by despite the FBI forcing them into exile, despite being wanted for a murder he never had anything to do with.

They sat at that table on the patio now several years into their exile. They had just returned from one of their musical tours in Africa, richer and more famous, but both of them depleted and anxious to chill in their home overlooking the sea. The breezes on the patio came from two different places. It was either off the sea below, in which case you could smell and even almost taste the salt water of the Mediterranean; this breeze was from that fertile basin where so many great cultures started and continued to the present moment. It was a breeze of culture and art, words on the page that formed into poetry, of dance and the operatic voice, and flamenco music. The other breeze came in off the land, back down in the Sahara, that great expanse of desert where only a few clever groups were able to survive. That breeze had its culture, too, but it was not laced with words or dance movements; it was a breeze of dry capability, a wind of fortune and tragedy, the wind that reduced men and women to migrainous headaches and anxieties, a breeze of calculation. It smelled of camel dung, desert springs, thick woolen cloth that ironically kept one cool in the desert. But salted into that southernly breeze was a new kind of possibility, the new world scraping away the old order; that was the smell of Africa scenting the wind, the smell of commerce, true, but also seeded with the music of a continent. Africa was music, if it was anything, how people talked, how they walked, it was all a kind of music, so that the scents and the tastes, the smells and the touch, all of it was part of that African music, and Algiers was its most northern point, a point of need, it was true, but also a point of this African possibility. There was no line in the sand where Africa ended and Northern Africa began. Algiers was as much a part of it as was Bamako.

"Do you know what James Joyce's father said at the end of his life?" Santiago asked Eileen.

"No, I don't, Santa, tell me."

"He said that he lived a life as good as a white man."

"We are the blacks of Europe. That's what Roddy Doyle says in *The Commitments*."

"No, I'm the black of Europe. You're the redhead of Europe. There is a difference."

"What would that be?"

"I can be shot for just walking down a street."

"I could be shot too."

"But the difference is that if you were shot, it is probably because you pissed off someone, you did something, or you didn't do something that you were supposed to. But with me, with me, I just have to walk down the street, the crime is my being Black, and I have that bullseye on my back, just for being who I am, not for anything I ever did to anyone."

"It's a very unfair world," Eileen said.

"And yet it is beautiful."

"It is beautiful," she repeated him, almost like a refrain in a blues song.

"Ugly beauty," he said, referencing his old friend Thelonious Monk, as he and Eileen walked, arm in arm, quietly and slowly along the edge of their gigantic patio overlooking the Mediterranean Sea.

Most of Santiago's concerts were in Africa, a continent full of new, liberated countries. In the 1970s, Europe lost its grip on these countries. There was a lot of hope in the air, and part of that hope was transmitted by Santiago Santa's music. He would play concerts in massive fields or in soccer stadiums. The places where he did this included Mali, Ivory Coast, Guinea, Nigeria, Ghana, South Africa, Zimbabwe, Tanzania, and Kenya. He even played concerts in the Sudan, Ethiopia, and Somalia. The Santas were part of the spectacle in Kinshasa, Zaire when Ali and Foreman fought "the Rumble in the Jungle" on October 30, 1974.

"Ali fought one of the greatest planned fights of all time, knocking out the seemingly invincible Foreman in the Eighth Round. The rope-a-dope," Santa said, pretending to shadow box.

Eileen feinted and jabbed back at her husband.

Santiago said, "Irish people are crazy for a fight."

"Don't fuck with me," Eileen said. "I'm Irish."

"Me too," he said. "I'm black Irish—only the real kind—like Ella and Billie."

"And I'm fake," she said. "Wind me up and watch me speak with me brogue."

Living in Algiers wasn't so bad, he said. He was known to the government and anyone who mattered in Algeria. He was a kind of asset, a chip the government held in case they needed to cash it in. After all, he was a famous piano player and composer, a radical Black American, like that other fellow exiled Black American in Algeria, Eldridge Cleaver, who now was so paranoid, he refused to see his old friend Santiago Santa, fearing that Santa was the man. That he was working for Uncle Sam as an agent provocateur. In the early days in Algeria, Santa saw Cleaver regularly; they had coffee in a downtown café. Though it was no longer French, Algiers was Mediterranean, but no one would ever mistake it for the Riviera.

Eldridge lived up in the hills too; he lived at a place they called The Embassy, where all the exiled black revolutionaries would gather. In the 1970s, Algiers was considered the capitol of the Third World. People knew that Franz Fanon had lived there ten or fifteen years earlier. They knew that at least at first the Black Panthers were considered another aspect of, if not the Oomah, than the New World Order. The Embassy was where you met and spoke with the Black Americans who were part of this revolutionary world.

When Eileen ran at four in the morning, no one was out on the streets. She wore the skullcap or had on the hoodie, and no one seemed to notice that she was a woman. There were other runners in those days, so they looked after her and sometimes ran with her and they knew who her husband was. Mostly Eileen ran by herself, solitary and unique, and she even stopped with the cigarettes, cutting it down from eighty to sixty to forty to twenty, and then halved it to ten, then five, and then zero. How she decided that nine miles was her daily run, even Eileen was not sure, but she seemed easily to accomplish that distance in an hour and a half, plus the fifteen minutes warming up and fifteen warming down, making it a two-hour experience daily. There was nothing much else to do. When the sun was up, it was too intense to do anything, except maybe in the dead of winter, when the world of Algiers might cool down a little. Algeria was not a place full of a lot of trees, she noticed, so there was no shade to seek out, only the glaring light of the sun and the white buildings, the tawny colors of the desert to the south, and the blue-green of the Mediterranean which they took in panoramically from their terrace.

Through the Seventies, they had struggled on and off with drugs and alcohol, the two ways they dealt with the loneliness of their lives and their exile. Within a few months of living in Algeria, they discovered that they could slip in and out of Tangier, not far away, with little or no fanfare. They used Irish passports, his via his grandparents on his mother's side. They would spend a month or two in Morocco after his concert tours, smoking hash or kief, sometimes using heroin *recreationally*, he called it. That's how he first shot up Eileen, and she liked it, she said, and wanted more.

"You're a pig for this stuff," he said one day, and she was, but she didn't care. A month or two in Tangier and she was strung out, and so was he.

Back in Algiers, they detoxed. A doctor whom they knew gave them drugs to withdraw off the heroin, and within a few weeks they were clean and sober again until the next big tour.

By the Eighties, they hadn't been to Tangier for some time, and had been clean for maybe two or three years. He still drank once in a while, and so did Eileen, her drinking a bit more dramatic and steady than Santiago's.

Things were not bad in 1980. The country was more stable than in the early 1970s. People had gotten used to both of them, though Eileen still did not know many people, only a handful of women she had met at the university. They were usually the wives of professors, even one or two professors themselves, one a medical doctor, another one who taught Islamic law, her father having been one of the great Islamic scholars of the country.

An entrepreneur in Tanzania wanted to book Santiago into a series of concerts and Eileen was managing the details for her husband. She wanted to run some numbers and details by Santiago, so she wandered into the back of their sprawling, one-story house towards the music studio and the gym. Santiago often spent long hours in the studio, recording and working on new pieces.

Eileen called out his name as she wandered down the hall. But she didn't get any answer. She saw a bathroom door slightly ajar, so she went towards it. He was slouched on the toilet seat with his trousers down around his ankles. A needle was stuck in his left forearm, and the capsule where the heroin had been was filled with his blood.

He had OD-ed on the toilet seat.

In the late 1960s, there were famous photographs that circulated widely in the music world of the comedian Lenny Bruce dead from an overdose in his bathroom, and later, thinking back on the scene, that's what it reminded Eileen of, the photographs of Lenny Bruce, dead, sprawled out, naked, in his bathroom, OD-ed.

Faced with the daunting task of saving her husband, Eileen had no time to think about anything else; she had somehow gotten him up and was trying to revive him by walking him around the studio. One of his arms rested on her shoulder and she grasped him by the waist. Before walking him, she managed to get his legs untangled from his trousers and had pulled the needle out of his arm. She walked him back and forth, talking to him all the time.

"Come on, Santa, don't let me down. Don't die on me in the middle of nowhere, and leave me a widow. Don't do that to me, man. Wake up. Come on, man, snap out of it."

He finally came around after she put some ice cubes down his underpants, and he snapped to.

"Fucked up," he said.

"You're telling me," Eileen answered. "Where did you get that shit?"

"Tangier," he said.

"And you didn't tell me?"

"I didn't," he said.

"Why?" she asked.

"I'm a junkie," he said.

"I thought we share everything," Eileen said.

"We do," Santiago answered. "We share everything."

BAMAKO

"To gain that which is worth having, it may be necessary to lose everything else."
—Bernadette Devlin

In the late autumn, the light was slant and sometimes golden, though mostly it was grey outside, and days were short and occasionally ominous, cold and damp. Eileen woke up and Santiago was on her mind. He wasn't there in the room, as he was at other times, but his presence hung over Eileen, like a rain cloud. She had an ache in the pit of her stomach or as she sometimes heard young people say, "There's a pit in my stomach," which was so wrong, it was right. She had a pain in that pit, but Eileen did not give in to the pain. Loss was loss, the darkness was real, she told herself, and yet she had to go on. At least you don't stay by yourself in a dark apartment with the curtains drawn and the lights out. So she got up and got dressed and went to the gym at 6:30 in the morning and then came back home, showered, and walked out the door around 9 a.m. Walking quietened the mind, and it was also a way to empty her head of miseries, moods, tensions, the old rigmarole of giving into her own personal despair, of making it into a palace in which, shoeless, she tiptoed into the grotto to worship what was no longer there, thus the despair. Self-pity was everywhere, and yet she knew that it had no business to be anywhere. Walking addressed that problem too. She walked in a straight up way, not bent over like some of the old ladies in her building; and Eileen had a stride to equal anyone's, covering great distances in one long step. Technically her boots were all wrong; she was wearing Frye cowgirl boots, hardly the best gear for hoofing around London, and yet it did not matter, nothing ever seemed to matter terribly much in the end, and when she was in this sort of mood, the end felt nigh.

Her legs hurt, so she thought the walk would do them good. She grabbed her old blackthorn walking stick and went down the gangway with a jaunty step, holding the blackthorn in her hand. It had a grand feel to it, the stick, and it steadied any wobble she had from the phlebitis in her legs. She left her sheltered accommodation on Hampstead Road and walked south towards the Euston Road and an overpass that bridged Tottenham Court Road with the street on which Eileen lived. Somewhere in this new array of signs and postings, street paintings of new lanes and old ones that came to an end, she managed to get herself across the busy road and turned right into Warren Street, past the Tube station and walked down the street. She crossed Warren and stepped into a tiny general store that sold international newspapers and magazines, among other things, and bought a newspaper, which she tucked under her arm, went out back to Warren Street and headed west for two blocks where she saw an opening to enter onto Fitzroy Square, a small elegant Georgian space designed by architect Robert Adam, all of the original houses still there, making it an architectural wonder that

London had not cherry-picked its houses to introduce new styles through the decades and centuries.

The city suddenly got quiet because there were no cars or lorries in the square at that moment, not that the cars and lorries couldn't drive there—they could—only the roadway, cobbled and made to seem inaccessible, was not inviting to traffic and so often it stayed away, with the odd exception of builders and delivery vehicles that would drive anywhere they could as long as no coppers gave them summonses for parking illegally.

Eileen sat down on a bench in front of her NHS surgery because she was early for her appointment. She happened to have purchased an *International Herald Tribune* for some exorbitant fee and was reading it as she waited for the doctors' office to open.

A tramp sat down next to her, even though there were other empty benches nearby.

"The second Duke of Grafton acquired the land," he said.

He wore beat up Doc Martins on his feet, fingerless gloves, an overly sized Scally cap on his head, and inhabited an enormous green military jacket with lots of pockets that he must have found in a charity shop. He smiled and showed that half his teeth were missing.

Eileen realized that he was familiar, though she could not put her finger on it just yet. Then it occurred to her who he was; he was a tramp who had been loitering in Tolmers Square for the past several months. In a closed area, his smell would put her in a twist, but since she had taken Ivermectin for the strongyloides, she had no smell, and outside on the park bench, the hum coming off of him was not objectionable. She hardly noticed it at all.

His friends were nowhere to be seen, but he had his usual sartorial flare combined with his messiness and devil-may-care attitude. She hadn't a clue who the Duke of Grafton was or why the tramp was banging on about him, but the hotel on TCR was called the Grafton and the nearby street had the same name, so Eileen presumed that Lord Grafton had something to do with this square.

"It was the Baron of Southampton who actually developed it," he went on.

"Excuse me," Eileen said.

"The bloody square," he said, waving his arm magnificently. "It's the Fitzroys I'm going on about, lovely."

"Ah, the Fitzroys," Eileen said, and went back to reading the *International Herald Tribune* in which she came across an article by one Mickey Mack Coole about Korea. He must be a relative, she thought. There are so few Cooles in the world.

"Meant to provide London residences for the filthy rich aristos," he said.

"I'm sorry," Eileen said. "I'm waiting for the doctors' surgery to open."

"Was built in four stages," he went on, ignoring her remark. He pointed to the two houses that were owned by an ex-husband of Madonna's. "Robert Adam built those on the south side and the east. His brothers finished the task in 1798."

If you can't beat him, Eileen thought, join him.

"What's that stone?" she asked, pointing to the fronts of the buildings.

"Originally *bloody* Portland stone," he said. "But the facades were *fecking* ruined during the Second World War, and were rebuilt more along the lines of the buildings in stucco on the north and *fecking* west sides of the square. The *fecking* Napoleonic wars made a balls of everything even earlier. It took years before work commenced again in *eighteen-twenty-and-catch-a-cold* and then the final phase in 1930 and likewise catch-a-*fecking* cold."

The surgery had opened, alas, and Eileen stood to go.

"It's been a pleasure," she said, lying, but before she got very far, her new friend said, "I read it all in the Wikipedia."

"Brilliant," she said. Then he shouted at her:

"Do you have a few million you can lend me?"

"See me next week," she called back.

"Same time, same place, next week," he shouted.

After the doctor's appointment, Eileen came out into Fitzroy Square, but she did not see the man with all the knowledge of the square anywhere in its four points. Even before the tramp had referenced Wikipedia, Eileen had gone there herself to read about the square. On one side of Fitzroy Square, the painter Whistler had lived, and no one conjured the moody crepuscle of a London evening as well as James McNeil Whistler. In more recent times, the famous writer Ian Whatshisname lived next door to

Nigella the famous cook and her enormously wealthy and fat husband who, Eileen noticed, lost a lot of weight the moment he ditched the famous cook.

She walked away from her NHS doctors' surgery, people coming in and out of the enormous doors. The surgery was next to a house once peopled by the likes of George Bernard Shaw and years later, Virginia Woolf, a Bloomsbury workshop just adjacent to their pile and where they no doubt carried on with each other as those folks often did. It made Eileen smile for the first time that day. She turned down the little spur of Grafton Way in the direction of Cleveland Street filled with interesting little shops and restaurants. She stepped across Cleveland where there were very few cars at that hour and headed into the stationer's, something she did every Monday around this time of morning.

The shop was owned by a South Asian family and it was usually the daughter who greeted Eileen, the parents in the back attending to their printing and copying business.

"I have some *clairefontaine* notebooks from France," the daughter happily declared to Eileen.

The daughter knew her customers because Eileen had stopped in for two things she could not do without, one of them being the *clairefontaine* notebooks, 80 pages, 40 sheets, 17 x 22 centimeters, usually 99 pence. The other thing that Eileen could not do without were refills for her Lamy fountain pen.

"Perfect," Eileen said.

She purred it like a St. Ives person might, caressing the syllables and vowels perfectly.

Perfect!

She grabbed several of the notebooks, one red, one green, one blue, and then located the ink cartridges for her pen.

"I can't survive without my French notebooks and my German ink cartridges," Eileen said.

"We are here to serve you," the daughter said, smiling.

"Oh, yes, I also need some lead for a pencil," Eileen said, more to herself, and went back to where they were located and grabbed a small container with the 7 mm lead.

And while she was at it, she bought several glue sticks, one small, one medium, and one large, all of which would be put to good use when she made her collages in the evening, after the writing had ended for the day.

She went to the counter to pay.

"We are going out of business," the young woman declared.

"When?" Eileen asked.

"End of month."

"Say it isn't so."

"It is so," the daughter said.

"Why?"

"Rents," the daughter said. "We can no longer sustain our shop."

"How long were you here?"

"Twenty years in this location," the daughter said, "and twenty in the one across the road and down the Cleveland Street."

The daughter wrote up the purchase by hand, tallied the costs, and rang up the transaction on the cash register. Eileen paid with a debit card because Monday was the day she got her weekly pension credit, which was now one-hundred-and-fifty pounds, deposited directly into her bank account.

Monday was always a day for extravagances, usually two or three things, maybe four if she were going to Waitrose or Sainsbury's. Nearly every Monday she stopped into this shop on Cleveland Street. Once she got to Marylebone, she might stop into Pret and get a sandwich and a tea or wait until after the meeting and have a sandwich at Bonne Bouche with some of the regulars, her crew from Hinde Street.

The daughter attempted to put the things in a paper bag, but Eileen grabbed everything and put them into her fishing tackle bag, a green canvas thing that she carried on her shoulder, and one which she had since her first arrival in London, having purchased it, a Shakespeare bag, at the tackle shop on Malden Road when she first stayed with Carmel on Savernake in Gospel Oak.

Now Eileen was walking again.

This time she only had to take a few more steps before she got to Clipstone and turned that corner, heading west again. She walked past a Banksy art piece of a rat that was painted on a wall and now had a Perspex window across the work to protect it from the depredations of Fitzrovia.

She walked past the council estate and then headed towards Great Portland Street. Across the road there was a sign advertising for the legal offices of Mark Coole, QC, a prominent silk, and every time she saw the sign she told herself that if she ever needed a QC, she would call him, who was a big, well-dressed, handsome fellow whom she frequently saw on the television news talking about human rights, something he cared about when he was not making millions representing celebrities in the courts of law down by the Strand and Fleet Street.

On Great Portland, if time allowed, Eileen stepped into Villandry to purchase a croissant to take with her and eat later in the morning when she became peckish. If time did not allow this stop at Villandry, an enormous and appealing bistro, she would return this way several hours later and maybe stop for a tea and some carrot cake. But today she would buy the croissant and then, after paying, leave the bistro and cross the street and go onto New Cavendish, walking ten short blocks (Duchess, Weymouth, and Mansfield, where a wealthy African student at University College London had turned to terrorism only to set his underpants on fire on a plane to the United States, and his bomb fizzled out, then Harley, Wimpole, Marylebone Mews, Westmoreland, Welbeck, etc.), until she came to Marylebone High Street.

If time allowed, Eileen turned right and walked north up the High Street to either Daunt bookshop or the Oxfam bookstore. (This was when it still was a good bookstore which it wasn't anymore, though Daunt remained superb.) Daunt was always good to walk into. If she had money in the bank or didn't have a shitload of bills to pay later in the week, she bought books or ordered them if what she wanted was not in stock. When broke, she dreamed of books she would purchase when money came her way once again. Now that she was past her 69th birthday, once a year in April, Eileen received a small pension from the Royal Literary Fund; it was run by another Eileen, this one named Gunn, whom Eileen Coole thought of as her guardian angel.

Where New Cavendish met Marylebone High Street, Eileen thought of that intersection—the word of the moment—as a kind of magic juncture, a nexus, like a sacred druidic mount in Ireland. It seemed as though all she had to do was think of someone, and they appeared on that corner. Sacred Celtic mound of New Cavendish and High Street, conjure for me, she prayed. She tried conjuring Santiago, and he did not so much appear as this young man walked into Eileen, and he was Santiago's spitting image. But instead of Santiago's wonderful educated Brooklyn accent, the young man had an East London accent. He apologized for bumping into her and trotted off towards Marylebone Road to the north.

Eileen had not seen her friend Will Neary, the actor, so she thought of him. He was as big as instant coffee these days, his face everywhere. He did commercials on television, and he was the star in lots of movies, and even though he was Irish, people said that he was Britain's favorite actor. Eileen and Will went back to her university days in Dublin. When he was not making a film, Eileen saw him at the central London meetings. So she closed her eyes and said, spirit of New Cavendish and Marylebone High Street, make Bill the actor appear.

And he did!

There he was, wearing his signature blue suit with suede loafers and colorful socks, and since it was a bit chilly out, he had on a cottony looking black rollneck and wore what looked to be a navy blue cashmere overcoat, smoking a cigarette and seeming as elegant as any human being could possibly be. Around his neck he wore a grey cashmere scarf, tied in a hangman's knot.

"Bill!" Eileen screamed. "I just conjured you and there you are!"

"Is that how I wound up here? I was just making a film in India and then suddenly I'm back on Marylebone High Street."

"How are you?" she asked.

"Darling Eileen, I'm the one who should be asking you that question."

He offered his hand to shake. He was not a hugger. The Irish never were. When you knew Bill, he offered you his hand. What made it unusual is that he had the Viking claw in which his pinkie and ring finger retracted back towards the palm, so when he shook your hand, it was with his thumb, index and middle fingers.

Eileen knew the drill, having shook his hand a thousand times, and just went with the flow at this druidic corner. Ireland's greatest actor Will Neary; Ireland's least-known woman poet, Eileen Coole. The energy was sensational, she thought.

"I thought maybe you moved back to Ireland," Bill said.

"That will never happen, Bill."

"Why?"

"Ireland is not my thing, Neary," Eileen said. "It was never my thing."

"The Church is less powerful nowadays; the government is one of the most progressive in the west."

"It's a long story," Eileen said.

"It always is," he laughed.

"True, true," Eileen whispered.

"Where have you been?" he asked, although she had been there, on that corner, nearly every Monday since she could remember.

"Here I am," she said.

Eileen towered over Bill. He projected a tall, thin elegance on the screen, but he was only about five feet seven inches tall, and Eileen was still her Amazonian six feet.

"Clean and sober and still holding onto London by my bedsit," Eileen declared, quoting a poem by a friend she knew in Hampstead.

"I love your humor," he said.

"I love you," she declared, and that was a bit too much for Bill, so he bowed in a courtly way and told Eileen that he would see her shortly at the Hinde Street meeting which was a half block and just a half-hour away from its start-time.

Bill walked off in the direction of Pret, where he would get a tea before the meeting.

Eileen headed in the opposite direction, towards the meeting on Hinde Street.

Because it was Monday, the meeting in the little room commenced at eleven o'clock, but in order to get a seat, she had to be there a half hour before, which Bill and Eileen usually were. But since he was off getting his tea at Pret, she put her jacket on the chair next to hers to save for Bill.

"No saving chairs," an old-timer said.

"I'm not," Eileen fibbed. "Bill just stepped out to get something."

"Bill is back from India?"

"He's back," she said, and the old-timer forgot about his complaint.

There were not supposed to be any food or drink in the meeting, but everyone ignored the rule, although once or twice a year the church sent someone down to the little room to read them the riot act, and for a few weeks, no one brought food or drink into the room. That was not the case that morning. All about Eileen people drank their lattes and cappuccinos and nibbled on Pret sandwiches. Eileen got out her Villandry croissant and ate it discreetly. Bill came in saying hello to everyone and settled next to Eileen.

"Let me buy you a tea afterwards," he said.

"It's my turn," Eileen told him. "Meet me at Bonne Bouche."

Bonne Bouche had no seating inside, but there were a row of chairs and tables outside under a canopy, and people sat out there year-round, rain or shine, winter or summer, smoking and chatting away.

If no one was free on a Monday, Eileen sat outside by herself, no longer a smoker, but enjoying the air and bustle of central London, which she seemed never to get tired of. If time allowed—and usually it did—where was she going, after all?—Eileen might stop into the charity shop next to Bonne Bouche and look around at the plates or the used clothing. Sometimes she wandered across the street and went to the Wallace Collection, just steps away.

"There's a story I want to tell you about my latest shoot," Bill said to Eileen, but just then the meeting was called to order and the room grew quiet and everyone stopped what they were doing to pay attention to the person leading the meeting.

"To be continued," Bill said.

After tea with Bill, Eileen walked back to her flat via the same route as she went to Marylebone High Street, and just before she got to Tottenham Court Road, she remembered that she needed a few items at the larger Sainsbury's. Her legs were hurting, but luckily she had left home with her blackthorn walking stick, which she leaned on, waiting for the street's walk sign to change in her favor, so that she could cross the road amid the crowded traffic on TCR. Once she entered Sainsbury's near the University Hospital, Eileen got herself a blue plastic shopping basket and marched to the back of the store. There she came upon Malik, who worked in frozen foods. A young man from Guinea in the west of Africa, he wore an orange Sainsbury fleece jacket year-round, along with gloves, a scarf, and a hat. "Like all West Africans," he said, "I have adjusted, I'm flexible." With that remark, he smiled shyly back at Eileen.

"Are you all right?" she asked.

"Am I all right," said Malik. "What happened to you?" He pointed to the blackthorn stick.

"Phlebitis," she said. "I'm getting old."

"You're not old," Malik said. "You are still beautiful."

Malik knew Eileen's backstory, the years of exile in the Maghreb, the tours that Santiago Santa did throughout Africa. He had even attended a big outdoor concert that Santa gave in Conakry, the capital of Guinea. Later, Malik would earn a scholarship to study science in London. But then he ran out of money and took a job working at Sainsbury's. That was almost a decade ago. It was much further back in time when Malik had attended Santiago Santa's concert while still a student in primary school. About that concert in Conakry, Malik often told Eileen how important it had been.

"It changed my life," he once told her after Eileen told him who her late husband was.

"Thank you," Eileen said.

It was almost as if Eileen were thanking him for Santiago.

"'No Justice / No Peace,'" Malik said. "That is the greatest piece of music ever written."

Malik had bloodshot, malarial eyes, and he shivered, working in the frozen food section of the supermarket on Tottenham Court Road. It was around zero Centigrade where he worked, even outside the freezers. Seeing Malik had revived some ancient memories in Eileen, replacing one illusion for another. Eileen and Santiago had departed from Algiers wearing safari clothes, looking like inexperienced tourists, not the seasoned travelers they were. She had on a linen shirt, a linen safari jacket, her jeans, her boots, and carried her leather jacket that she wore only in the Land Rover when the air-conditioning got too cold. Once they were out in the desert the air conditioning in the SUV never felt too cold, though; instead a kind of malaise set in, the heat grinding them down in its intensity. This gig in Bamako was very important; they had been promised the money before the concert, and that money would get them to their other gigs in the nearby countries.

She hadn't really prepared for the journey through the Sahara. She thought it might be a day or two. But it went on and on, the heat unbearable, even the air-conditioned SUV unbearable. Their driver and guide got them to an oasis for the night. There were palm trees, water to drink, a place to bathe.

The first driver signed off once he delivered them to the oasis. The next driver was more local; he had none of the city sophistication of the first driver.

The Land Rover opened out into a giant tent which the Santas slept in. They invited their new driver to join them, but he was too shy and slept away from their tent, under a palm tree.

Eileen drank tea as Santiago nursed his beer.

"Remember that Jesuit?" Santiago asked.

"Who?"

"Tom."

"Bill."

"Yes, Bill."

"Old Bill."

"Yes. The fellow in London."

"He took us to lunch at his rectory in Mayfair. He was a character, that one."

Old Bill was also from Dublin, which is how Eileen had first met him, through a mutual friend in London.

"When you asked him how he was, do you remember what he would say?" Santiago questioned her.

"*Terribly well,*" Eileen said, conjuring Old Bill through her mimicry.

"Is that how you are?"

"No," Eileen said. "I'm feeling terribly awful."

"I like your stick," Malik said. Then he laughed. "What a foolish thing to say." And he laughed again, as if in some existential moment, he stood outside this scene and looked upon it compassionately but with humor, and at great remove.

"It was me granddad's blackthorn," said Eileen.

"Is it Irish?"

"Of course it's *fookin'* Irish, Malik."

He laughed once more.

"It looks very African."

"It has a lot of juju and mojo," she told him.

There was a pause, as there often was, as Malik formulated some English words in his head to exchange with his friend Eileen Coole.

"How old are you now, Eileen?"

"Now that's a terribly unkind thing to ask an old woman. But if you have to know, I'm seventy," she said. "Well, I'll be seventy on 16 June."

Malik was not tall and he had a slight build and his dark skin was chalky, ruddy and pocked on the cheeks and his forehead. His hair was worn short, but he had a slight pompadour. He was not a handsome man, and yet there was something appealing about his look, perhaps because he seemed to exude compassion for other people. He once told Eileen that he was a Sufi, which explained his serenity and balance.

Eileen first met him in Sainsbury's as Malik helped someone from her building, an old woman who hobbled about using a Zimmer frame with a cloth shopping bag tied to it. Malik ran around the supermarket getting things the old woman needed. Eileen also saw him help other people from her building, her friend Dickie Farrell, Tanya the Greek lady, and so many others, including the grumpy Mr. Murphy.

"When you say that you are almost seventy years old, I cannot believe my ears, Eileen Coole. You have the vitality and beauty of a far younger woman."

"Go on now," she said. "Me legs are going." Then she changed the subject. "Do you hear anything from home?"

"Everyone knows someone who has died in the last

few months," he said, not matter-of-factly, but with a lot of emotion, his face straining to contain itself.

"In your family?"

"God is good," he said, "no one in my family. But everyone knows of a neighbor or a former classmate or someone you once worked with."

Malik seemed more like a Buddha than this odd mixture of Sufism, the Sunni version of Islam, and his own native animist beliefs.

"One day I will have my own blackthorn walking stick," he said.

He smiled dreamily.

Eileen told him that she would keep an eye out for one. She warned him not to go down to New Oxford Street and pay the full shilling for a new one in the umbrella shop at the end of Gower Street where the buses seemed to congeal at any time of day or night.

"They'd charge you an arm and a leg, Malik."

"Bloody hell," he said, a phrase he had picked up from Eileen over the years.

"Bloody hell is right," said Eileen. "Now let me do me shopping, Malik, before I forget what I came here for."

"A good day, Eileen, a good day to you. May peace be yours."

"You're a most kind fellow, Malik. I will pray for your friends and family that they will not get sick."

"I am most grateful to you, Eileen Coole," he said, and he shuffled off to do his work of restocking the frozen foods in the large, efficient freezers at the back of the supermarket.

Eileen hobbled off on her old junkie legs, leaning on her blackthorn stick, looking for the Jarlsberg cheese, whose label said it was made to "a secret Norwegian formula" in Ireland. Reading that label, it was perhaps the only time Eileen thought of leprechauns and the good people whilst still living in contemporary London. She saw them churning butter somewhere outside of Roscommon, then using the secret Norwegian formula, the end result being these lovely packages of Norwegian cheese from Ireland, which happened to be her favorite choice when she shopped.

She then looked for some Earl Grey tea, the Taste the Difference 50 tea-bag pack, and some soy milk. She placed a package of two small Ciabattas that were still on sale for half price into her basket, and she selected some tomatoes, lemons, broccoli, and a large bottle of Evian water. The water and the soy milk added weight to the groceries, so she scooted along with her stick in one hand and her shopping basket in the other.

Instead of thinking about Santiago and that trip to Bamako, she remembered that day, more than ten years earlier, after she had lost her teaching job at Surbiton University, and when she had gotten misdirected by the Citizens Advice Bureau on the high street in Kilburn which wound up making her fight, for many years, a losing battle in the courts. She had learned that the courts were not so much about justice as they were about maintaining the status quo. She remembered another visit to Sainsbury's—not this one but the one in Kilburn—and how she had packed her basket with food and sundries she had purchased in the Kilburn Sainsbury's. But then the card was rejected. That would not happen today, she reckoned, as there was money in her account, not a lot, but enough to pay her rent, the utilities, and buy groceries when she needed them, though not much left over for anything else. It was that old adage that the Higher Power took care of your needs, though not necessarily your wants and desires.

Before Santiago died, he assured Eileen that she was going to survive all right after he was gone. He had begun to receive his royalties from his record sales, and he believed that it would flow to Eileen steadily. But once he died, a lawyer in New York managed to re-direct all the income from his music to an account held by Santiago's ex-wife in New Mexico and their daughter in Brooklyn, and Eileen never saw a penny of it from that point onward.

As she walked up and down the aisles in the back of the store, she thought of all the different languages Malik spoke, including French, English, Italian, Spanish, and Portuguese, but also some Pular, Manika, Susu, Kissi, Kpelle, and Loma, and that Malik, unlike sixty percent of his countrymen, was literate, and had even been to university in England.

The world he had left behind in western Africa was one of bauxite, diamonds, gold, and now oil, of amazing stretches of interior that were forested and contained unusual African animals. If Malik were a woman in

Guinea, he would be married while in his teens, and if he were a prostitute, two out of every five of them had AIDS. If Malik were a woman, it might mean he had a fifty/fifty chance of being in a polygamous marriage. Everyone had malaria; it came with the territory. Malik certainly had it, or at least his eyes suggested that he did. Eileen had it too. But Guinea also had Ebola, and several thousand people had succumbed to it in Malik's hometown, though no one in Malik's family, only his neighbors and former classmates, even some of them who had become doctors and nurses.

Eileen saw him at the back of the store as she stood looking at the smoked salmon or for something on sale. He waved goodbye to her and went off behind a closed door at the back of the store. She walked stiffly towards the self-checkout, and after ringing up her items, she stuffed everything into a canvas bag she bought a few years earlier from Planet Organic, not in Bloomsbury just down the road, but up in Muswell Hill where she went one morning to buy art supplies, taking the 134 bus across the road from her flat, which deposited her right in front of the Planet Organic.

When Eileen found herself at the oasis in the desert she was thirty-four years old, and as she told Santiago, "my biological clock is ticking loudly." Santiago was in his mid-fifties.The Santas had lived in Algiers for over ten years. Often they flew to destinations where Santiago was to perform. This time, instead of flying, they wanted to cross the Sahara in a Range Rover. They hired a guide from a travel bureau in Algiers, with the assignment for him to deliver them to the oasis, where another guide would take them to Mali. The new guide came from Ziza. During that journey across the Sahara, Santiago was sick. But Eileen was sicker. As her biological clock ticked away, the sands were running out of the hour glass. They had traveled from Algiers through the Atlas Mountains and into the Sahara without incident, except for a flat tire in Ziza, which their toothless emaciated driver got fixed in no time because he was from those nearby hills and mountains. But neither Santiago nor Eileen had ever experienced the heat of the desert quite this way or at least had not experienced the humidity-less heat of the Sahara, which was deceptive and finally overpowering. Previously, they realized now, they had thought they had been to the desert, but actually they had been to the desert's edge, a quite different thing than being deep into the center of the Sahara. They thought they knew heat, but they had no idea how dizzying and disoriented the desert heat made people who were not from there. The desert took over your mind, leaving you listless and unclear, even though they were in the Land Rover with its seemingly cool interior. The Land Rover was no match for the desert.

The journey from Algiers took almost a week.

Once they crossed the border into Mali, first Santiago, then Eileen, complained of dizziness, headache, and stomach pains. They stopped in Tombouctou to reconnoiter and get their bearings. Their Algerian driver was replaced with yet another one from Mali.

The SUV pointed towards Bamako, which they hoped to reach before nightfall. But perhaps that was a bit unrealistic. It might be a day or two more before they got to Bamako.

Every bump and rut in the roadway seemed to upset Eileen. So did the clothing she had to wear, having changed into a burqa somewhere in the Sahara and stowing the linen jacket and the jeans for another part of Africa.

"For fuck sake," she muttered, behind her burqa, her green-green eyes and her pale-pale skin poking out.

Santiago wore an expensive pair of khakis, a safari jacket, and a Panama hat. He smoked nervously as they went from seeing no people in the desert to seeing nothing but people beyond the windscreen in Mali.

"We'll get you to the hotel," Santiago said, "and you'll feel better, Eileen."

"I'm going to die," she said.

"Now, now," he said.

"For fuck sake, Santiago," she muttered.

Her Irish speech sounded so odd in Mali, far more than even his Brooklyn accent that even his wonderful education could not completely erase.

Their new driver was younger and friendlier, and he knew his way around Mali. He was from Bamako, he said.

"No worries, boss," he pronounced to Santiago.

"No problem," Santiago Santa said, a phrase he picked up from Chicago jazz musicians when they played with his groups.

"For fuck sake," Eileen whispered, almost like a prayer.

"Does he have to hit every rut in the *feckin'* road?"

Their driver spoke to them about kola nuts, and how they used to be currency, and about cotton, gold, and salt. "He's a poet," Santiago said. The driver went on to speak about Islamic scholars who were a big part of Mali. What was Santiago doing in Mali?

"I'm going to play a gig with Ali Farka Touré," Santiago said.

There was a pause. The driver seemed to be thinking.

"Are you Santiago Santa?"

Santiago nodded.

"I have t'ree of your albums, sir."

"That's grand," Santiago said, sounding a bit like Eileen now.

He had picked up that expression from Eileen over the years. Everything was grand in Eileen's world—until it wasn't. She was turning into her mother, she thought.

But their driver really was a poet. He went on:

"The Tuaregs of the Sahara, the Sonrai of Tombouctou, the Malinkes from the border regions of Bamako, the Dogon cliff dwellers, the Wassalous near the Cote d'Ivoire…"

"Yes, yes," Santiago nodded, feeling slightly better after they had stopped in Tombouctou, breaking the week they spent crossing the Sahara. "We have been studying all of these people."

"We have many ethnic groups," the driver said. "For instance, sir, there are the Falas of central Mali. Shall I drive you to the Hotel Wassulu?"

"Yes, yes," Santiago said.

Santiago lit a cigarette and offered one to the driver, who accepted it gratefully. Someone had brought Santiago a tin of Balkan Sobranies from London. They were deliciously smooth, the smoking of them.

"You must see the Grand Mosque whilst you are in Bamako," the driver said.

"We intend to visit it," Santiago told the driver.

"And the Central Market."

"Yes, yes, we will visit the market," Santiago told him.

"Is your wife all right?" the driver asked.

"I think Eileen will come around when we get there. She's just a little under the weather."

"I'm dying," she said from the back seat.

"She's dying," Santiago said.

"Yes, yes," the driver said, not fully understanding their words. He was not so much fluid in English, but that he was a good mimic from other English-speaking people he had driven around Mali.

By the time they got to Bamako, Eileen had lost the baby.

CUNNING

I had, it seems,
unknown to me,
been living my
life to the full.

—Dennis O'Driscoll

HAMPSTEAD ROAD

Two tramps were sat across from Eileen in the waiting room at the University College London Hospital. They were clapped out, head to toe, and they had a hum coming off their clothes, making it difficult to breathe in the room outside the Phlebotomy Department, where Eileen was also sat, only more anxious than most, as she had to have blood drawn. One tramp had on a dirty overcoat reaching almost to his ankles, and he wore one white trainer shoe and one black. The other tramp wore a raggedy tweed jacket which was accentuated by the filthiest scarf in the Western world. Eileen was not sure how much longer she could inhabit this sepulcher of odors in the otherwise spotlessly clean UCL Hospital, which was located at the juncture of Gower Street and the noisy, treacle of traffic and air pollution known as the Euston Road, with the train station just down the block and across the road from the hospital.

When Eileen's number came due, she sprang out of her chair faster than Hussain Bolt out of the starting blocks of a hundred meter race. A friendly, round-faced Asian woman greeted her. It was the phlebotomist. Eileen knew because she had gone to this one several times before.

Eileen rolled up her sleeve for the phlebotomist to put a rubber string around the forearm, and because Eileen had dealt with her before, she knew that the woman was a Filipina. The phlebotomist sighed upon seeing the condition of those tired veins.

"I'm clean," Eileen said.

"How long?"

"Twenty-five years."

"The wreckage of the past," the phlebotomist said.

"Better than the wreckage of the future."

Eileen smiled. She knew the drill. The phlebotomist looked for a good vein, would finally give up, and then she would use the one Eileen had suggested originally, the big vein at the top of her left hand, the only vein in her body still able to deliver vials of blood in no time.

After the bloodwork, Eileen went home to rest across the Euston Road from the hospital. She was exhausted, and it was only nine o'clock in the morning. She lay on her bed and fell asleep almost instantly; she did not wake up until around ten-thirty, refreshed and ready to face another day.

Someone knocked on the door and Eileen answered it. It was one of the temporary sheltered managers.

"All right?" the white-haired, harried, moon-faced woman in a blue tracksuit asked.

"Right," Eileen answered, and shut the door.

So much for interactions with the council. They wouldn't bother her again for another week.

After an elevenses of Earl Grey tea and some toast, she took a shower, got dressed and walked down through Bloomsbury, winding her way through its streets until she found herself on Marchmont, where she visited two bookshops, Judd Books and Skoob. Once she had enough of the bookshops, she walked to the end of Marchmont, past the Brunswick Centre, turned the corner and went into the Pret a Manger for a falafel sandwich and a green tea. After eating, Eileen read a little, then sauntered towards Russell Square.

Suddenly the sky opened up with a massive rain storm, so Eileen took cover in the Hotel Russell, waiting it out on the steps of the hotel. When she first came to London, this hotel had been called the Virginia Woolf, which was a name Eileen preferred to the Hotel Russell. Eileen did not sentimentalize London, but there were certain locations that bred a kind of nostalgia in her, and Russell Square was one of those places. She could not stand there on the rainy steps of the Hotel Russell and not imagine T. S. Eliot on the other side of the square, coming from Faber & Faber after a day's work and stopping into this very hotel to have a cocktail with his secretary Valerie, the young and future Mrs. Eliot.

As quickly as the rain came, it had gone, so Eileen stepped out into the breach of the day and proceeded onward.

The tourists were gone from the street because of the torrential rain, and there was a wonderful smell of wet earth in the air, reminding her of Ireland. Rain or shine, Russell Square gave Eileen a particular feeling not unlike an old beatnik might feel walking through Washington Square in downtown Manhattan. She could sense the ideals, the possibilities in this square, not just T. S. Eliot coming out of Faber's office over by SOAS and Birkbeck College, but 1960s peace marchers, University of London free-thinkers, pot smoke in the air, Allen Ginsberg chanting Om. This made Eileen recall, with great fondness, her meeting Ginsberg on East 10th Street in downtown Manhattan in 1966. What was that young poet's name who de-virgined her? His first name was Stan; but she could not remember his last name. Schwartz? Goldberg? Steiner? Did it even matter, as so much water had passed under that bridge.

Off in the distance, well beyond Russell Square, lightning struck somewhere, and Eileen shuttered. Like one of her heroes, James Joyce, Eileen Coole was deathly afraid of thunder and lightning.

Twenty years earlier, she heard a similar crack of thunder, only it was Algiers, where such a storm would be unusual, though not impossible to witness. But this sound was not from nature but man-made. It was a Friday, when the downtown mosque where Santiago often went was filled with worshippers coming to pray. Many died; hundreds were injured. It was the usual culprits, the Islamists, though in the early 1990s in Algeria, nearly everyone was an Islamist. They even believed that Santiago Santa was one, though Eileen knew that he wasn't. He was not even a Muslim; he just liked their sublime sense of social justice, something he shared with nearly everyone in Algiers at the time.

Santiago had gone to the mosque to meditate and pray with the others, mostly some professors he had befriended from the university. They often played tennis and afterward discussed philosophy and religion over mint tea and sweet biscuits.

He had already crossed the street from the mosque when the bomb went off.

The concussion from the explosion had blown him sideways across the hood of a parked car, and when he got home, the back of his head was covered in blood from the bits of glass, concrete and debris that had been thrown out from the explosion.

For days Eileen used tweezers to pick bits and pieces of concrete and glass from his shaven head.

He laughed as she picked the pieces from his skull with tweezers.

"You feckin' eejit," she said.

"I'm alive," he said, which was a good point.

Others were no longer alive.

But something happened from that day forward to both of them. Santiago sat and spoke with Eileen about her drug use.

"You should talk," she said.

"These Islamists are serious," he said. "I think we need to think about an exit strategy. I also think we need to get clean, both of us."

It was the first time he had admitted to her that he had a drug problem. Until that moment, it was always Eileen who had the jones, not Santiago.

"I'm thinking of Switzerland," he said.

"Switzerland?"

"There's a detox and rehab outside of Bern."

"Fuckin' Bern? Swiss cheese and cuckoo clocks, chocolate and yodeling."

"I'm telling you, Eileen, this is serious. We need to leave Algiers very soon."

This was around the time when Eileen's old graduate school friend Hugh Selwyn had advised the Santas to leave Algiers immediately. Hugh was a high up official in the American State Department's Africa desk. He knew what he was talking about, even though Santiago did not like or trust him at all.

"In this one instance," Santiago said, "I think your friend Hugh is right. We need to leave everything, pack up and go. There are going to be more bombs shortly. We are likely to get kidnapped and ransomed, and when they discover that no one wants to pay for us, they'll kill us and dump our bodies in the desert. I don't want to end up like Agamemnon, *dahlink*."

This was not a typical way that Santiago Santa talked; usually he was too lax, too easygoing about everything. He frequently called Eileen an alarmist when she reminded him where they were and what could happen to either of them. So on Santiago's instruction, Eileen contacted Hugh Selwyn of the American State Department, and her friend Hugh set in motion an emergency plan for exit from Algeria.

That evening, each of them packed one suitcase, leaving their books and CDs, their records and tapes, manuscripts of music and poetry, cookbooks, cooking utensils, clothing, shoes, and sunglasses. All the paintings on the walls and the sculptures on the garden terrace were left in place, making it appear that they were just going away briefly and would return. They only packed what they could fit into their own suitcases.

Santiago repeated an expression that he had only used once before when they fled from America in May 1970, after the shootings at Kent State and Jackson State.

"We're going to travel Indian style," he repeated it again.

"Only what we can place in the palm of a hand," Eileen answered.

"You got it, *girl*."

In 1970, they each packed a small suitcase, traveling in a manner that Santiago called "Indian style." Only what you could hold in your hand. The metaphor was still apt. Back then, they drove from Oakland down to the Mexican border, then onwards to Mexico City where they booked passage on a flight to Havana.

In Algiers in the early 1990s, someone lent Eileen a warm but beat-up tweed overcoat to wear, as they were transiting to Switzerland ultimately. She stood on the terrace looking out at the city of Algiers from their perch high up in the hills near the university. The Mediterranean was dotted with the lights of small boats, with the occasional ocean liner in the distance, appearing like a mirage on the horizon out of a Fellini film. Eileen cried as she looked at the view of the city and the Mediterranean from this angle for perhaps the last time in her life. Then she was ready to leave with Santiago.

A fellow named Abdul-Rahman arrived in a van late that evening; he had been sent to pick them up under instructions from Hugh Selwyn, Eileen's old friend. Abdul-Rahman drove them down to the waterfront.

They hopped in a small motorboat and then sped off into the Mediterranean Sea, searching for a larger boat offshore that was heading to Marseilles. From there, they flew to Switzerland.

The detox in Bern was not co-ed, so they didn't see each other for two weeks, but then met up again in the rehab, although they had to sleep in different wings of the clinic. Neither was in a particularly bad period of their addiction, and probably alcohol played a bigger role than heroin, because heroin was something they did when touring, not while living in Algiers. Alcohol could be bad enough in Algeria in those days, and if the Islamists found it in your possession, you could be arrested or worse. They might execute you on the spot, being an infidel, being a European, being Americans, being a jazz musician and his crazy Irish wife, being exiles, being cunning outsiders, being silent partners to everything that the Islamists were against, including democracy, European culture, jazz, rock 'n' roll, poetry books and novels, pork, friends with their enemies the Jews, enemies of their friends (the dictators in Africa); and finally Eileen Coole and Santiago Santa were not Algerian. They were an American and his Irish wife or, another way of putting it, a European woman with a black American husband. No, alcohol was verboten in Algiers in those days, and yet someone always had a way to get the odd bottle of Irish whiskey, red and white wine (by the case), even beer and Guinness once in a while.

Safe in Bern, they detoxed, using various prescriptions to bring them off the shelf of their addictions. Eileen was more cold-turkey than Santa, who had a relatively easy time of it once they administered the medications during the detox. In the rehab, he looked as good as ever, certainly he didn't look like a 65-year-old pensioner. He was still athletic and handsome. Eileen came into rehab gaunt and alabaster, her red hair untethered in multiple tendrils and coils, a mad Medusa. Usually Santiago was playful and whimsical with Eileen, but even Santiago Santa had that grim countenance of an addict on ice.

Eileen looked like hell, but was more or less all right, despite some liver dysfunction. Santiago still looked good, in spite of his addictions and other problems related to the addictions, including hepatitis. Once they were settled at the rehab in Bern, Santiago would learn that he was HIV positive.

She had loved Irish whiskey, and drank it like water.

"*Uisge beatha*," she said, "*the breath of life*: it runs in me veins."

"Do you have any veins left?" Santiago asked.

"You should talk," she said, punching him in the arm. She often did that to him when she was drunk. He said she had the punch of a Tommy Hearns. It was the Tommy Hearns who first fought Sugar Ray Leonard, not the Hearns of the Marvin Hagler or the Iran Barkley fights.

Eileen was pushing 45 years old when they came to Bern. There was no thought of *uisge beatha* or even a beer, much less getting a rig together and doing some horse. They really were going to wrestle their monkeys to the ground and execute them in Switzerland, in the snowy pureness of the Alps, amid the chocolate and cheese-eating yodelers and the profundity of Paul Klee's art.

"Switzerland," Eileen said, "where James Joyce, Tristan Tzara, and Vladimir Lenin would run into each other when they were out on their *passeggiata*."

"I don't think Lenin needed to detox," Santiago said, more grimly than usual.

The lightning had stopped and the sun came out before Eileen exited from the southwest corner of Russell Square, going up Montague Street towards the British Museum, and then down a side street to peak in the windows of the London Review of Books bookshop on Bury Place. She walked further on to New Oxford Street, and then into Covent Garden, just west of Gower Street, taking a side alley so that she came into the surround of Renzo Piano's colorful buildings across from St. Giles' Church. Piano's architecture brought this part of London back to life for Eileen. The colors invariably lifted her spirits. Of course, it might also be that she was moments from the churchyard across the road, and St. Giles was a church not for the well-heeled and trendy, but the indigent, the poor, especially streetwalkers and winos, i.e., it was Eileen's kind of church.

She might step into the courtyard from the front entrance of the church, in which case she could walk through the rear hall of the church to get to the inner courtyard and the building where she was heading. Or she could walk around the building on the right, going down the broken marble steps, and then circle back towards the inner courtyard and that discreet building behind the church where she intended to go. Or she could cross from the Piano buildings and enter a gate into the inner courtyard, going along the left side of the church, coming upon a pocket park.

Eileen chose the last way to walk.

She nodded hello to a few people whom she knew who were in the garden, the sun now out, they sat there eating lunch, on a balmy day in mid-December.

"Eileen!" a woman shouted. "Where the fuck have you been? I haven't seen your arse in ages."

"I'm here every week," Eileen said. "Where have you been?"

"South of France, darling. It was appalling, nothing but rain and Germans."

Eileen entered the one story building, walked down an ecclesiastical hall, and entered one of the most beautiful interiors in all of London. The room had high ceilings and was boxish without appearing to be so because of its enormous dimensions. A huge wooden table stood in the center of the room in front of an old fireplace. Portraits of previous vicars were over the fireplace and nearly all of the walls were painted in gold-leaf with names of various rectors, listed two at a time, like the animals on Noah's ark. The names dropped back along the walls into the early 17th century, but there had been a church at this site from the earliest 12th century and possibly back to the Romans.

Every Wednesday Eileen came here.

After the meeting, a bunch of people would go to the Jazz Café at Foyles, not the new location, but further north along Charing Cross Road, though that was now part of the history of the area, another part of it given over to development. Nowadays they had to make do with the nearby Starbucks or a Café Nero. Foyles had gone upmarket, moving several buildings south on Charing Cross Road, and the Jazz Café was no longer there. So they sat in a Pret a Manger and kibbutzed with one another.

They laughed; they talked, gossiped, told jokes, once in a while cried, laughed again and then went on their ways until the next week. After the meeting after the meeting, Eileen cut back around the Crossrail construction site, and then hoofed it up Tottenham Court Road with an old lady from Sligo, both of them whispering about Ireland, a country neither had spent much time in for forty or more years, except for the odd call upon family to celebrate a birth or death of some importance, usually a death that would not be covered over by a condolence card, email or telephone call.

The woman's name was Maeve, a down-on-her-luck nurse who had worked as a prostitute in Covent Garden before she got sober. She was 51 years old and had a bad heart, but was continually waiting for the NHS to do something about her condition. Nothing shocked her, which is why Eileen enjoyed her company, plus Maeve's speech was as foul as the weather, a most pagan and Celtic woman, even though it was a sunny day.

"A fella is sitting at the pub when his friend comes in and the other says to him, 'The Chinaman likes his bamboo,' finishes his pint and goes on his way. Years go by. The first fella is still sitting at the bar when the second one comes back in. It's been at least ten years. The first says to the other: 'Now what is it about the Chinaman and his bamboo that you were banging on about.'"

Maeve laughed so loud that people turned around to see what was going on.

Eileen smiled. Maeve had told her this same story several weeks earlier.

They stopped into Lil' Waitrose on Tottenham Court Road so that Eileen could buy salmon, a lemon, a small bottle of olive oil, and some broccoli for dinner. Then they walked up TCR until they came to Heal's and then Eileen scooted around the corner and went into Planet Organic to buy some Earl Grey tea.

Once they crossed Euston Road, Eileen said goodbye to Maeve, who turned towards King's Cross where she lived in a council flat.

"See you next Wednesday," Eileen said.

"Ta," said Maeve and wended off into the pedestrian traffic of people getting an early start on the commute to the Home Counties.

Maeve's ta reminded Eileen of Dickie Farrell, her neighbor, who always said goodbye that way. But it also reminded her of Santiago, who first said *ta* to her when they met bumping into each other at the Jazz Workshop in North Beach a lifetime ago. Santiago's *ta* to Eileen at the jazz club was what got her attention immediately, making her aware that this man was quite unusual, not your typical American at any rate, not even your typical jazz musician. Maeve's *ta* at first gave Eileen a burst of energy and a sense of well-being because it reminded her of Santiago Santa. But once the memory of him entered inside of her, that old ache of a loss and the endless cycle of grieving slid back into her being, and the pain of that loss was with her as she trudged towards her doorway on the noisy and busy venue known as Hampstead Road.

In the late afternoon of this short life, Eileen cooked her dinner, ate, then sat around polluting her mind with the *Evening Standard* which she had gotten from a hawker in front of the Warren Street Tube station across the road before coming home to her early evening meal.

By seven in the evening, the birds had stopped twittering on the balcony. The belch of traffic had subsided, though it was still all bustle on Hampstead Road.

Eileen thought of calling some people, then decided it was too late. She'd call tomorrow. Why do today what you can put off until tomorrow?

By eight, she was sat on the futon, reading a book, a collection of stories by William Trevor. She also was reading an essay on Dante by T. S. Eliot, a poem by a young

Irish woman whose work she did not know previously (the recommendation of a friend), a play by Tom Stoppard, a memoir by Joan Didion, a new book of stories by Alice Munro, a fat history book about the Mediterranean by Fernand Braudel, and another fat history book by Tony Judt on postwar Europe.

Eileen read unprogrammatically, like a magpie.

By nine, she had changed into a London Irish hoodie and techno workout trousers and was in bed but still reading. Lights out a few minutes later.

She was awakened several times in the night, once by drunken revelers, a nightly occurrence, several times by alarms (police, fire brigade, but mostly ambulances on the way to the hospital across the road).

"Never live across from a hospital again," she said to no one in the room, more as though spoken to the void around her. Perhaps it was addressed to the spirit of her late husband whose presence she often felt in the middle of the night.

When she couldn't sleep right away, she looked out the bedroom window at the December moon, amber and full.

Down below at the street level, some junkies congregated under the lamppost, nodding and conversing. In the past, she would call the police, but they never came or, if they did, they were hostile to Eileen for calling them. She had learned to be as wary of the police as she was of the resident junkies, who bred a false nostalgia in Eileen, a small, restless, irritable voice asking why she couldn't get high too. It would be different this time, the voice said.

But that was rubbish. It was never different, and she had been clean for more than twenty-five years, despite the NHS insisting on testing her now and then as though she had relapsed.

Around four in the morning, sleep had more or less evaded her, so she got up and went into the kitchen, turned on the overhead light and made herself a cup of tea and a piece of toast. She turned on her laptop computer.

It was already a new day, one many hours into its journey, leaving Eileen to wonder if she would ever catch up to it. As she sipped her Earl Grey tea, Eileen experienced something which had become familiar and regular an occurrence in recent years. She went from thinking about Santiago to being in the room with him.

"How are you, *dahlink*? he asked, using a fake Yiddish accent he sometimes affected when being cheeky and playful with her.

"I'm all right," Eileen said. "I'm fine."

"Fine?" he asked still affecting the Borough Park accent.

Eileen cried.

"Why did you have to die?"

"It happens to everyone, *dahlink*, didn't you get the memo?"

"Fucking *hell*, Santa," she said. "Bloody *fucking* hell."

"I'm all right," he said, and then he disappeared, gone as if for good.

Eileen was left by herself in the lonely rooms of her flat, a widow, still grieving a decade later, her medieval knees aching, her contemporary heart aching too. Her hands shook as she tried to sip the Earl Grey tea in her large white mug.

"Bloody fucking hell," she said.

A woman knows these things, Eileen thought. She senses it—intuits it. It is revealed to her in such a way. In Eileen's case, the way it was revealed to her was a revelation: they (the Santas) were living in Paris. They had escaped successfully from Algiers. A speedboat to a freighter, the freighter to the port of Marseilles; a journey through the Alps to Bern, and there a rehab for many months and much money later. A hotel in Paris: the Lenox, where they lived now and where he played most evenings in its intimate cafe. The Lenox, where Joyce wrote part of *Ulysses*, and its stairway where Eileen often encountered his spirit, incorporeal and delightful. He had begun to call her Lovely, as in: "Hello, Lovely." "Hello," she said. "I'm Eileen Coole." "I know who the *feck* you are," Joyce's spirit said. "I've been reading your poetry for years." It was in this context that Eileen confided to the Master, as she called him, usually communing with him as she went out of the Santas' hotel room, down the stairwell to the lobby. "It's my husband," she said. "Who?" "A musician," she said. "The only group more unsavory than writers," Joyce told her. "He's all right in that regard," Eileen said. "Then what is the trouble, Mizz Coole?" "Miriam," she said. "Miriam?" "One of his girlfriends." "Ah," Joyce said. His *ah* was filled with sympathy and compassion for Eileen.

As she wended her way down the winding staircase at the Hotel Lenox, Joyce walked along beside Eileen.

"At the end of their lives," Joyce said, "men and women are so different, and from what I am seeing, your husband, your partner, I think you 21st Century beings call them—I used to pretend that Nora was my wife, when she was also my partner…"

Joyce seemed to have lost the thread.

"Where was I, Coole?"

"Some malarkey about men and women being different."

"Ah," he said. "The mind, even in the afterlife, never stops processing qualia and the quotidian. But here is my point, Eileen Coole: men regret what they have done; women regret what they haven't done."

"You are still the wisest of people, Monsieur Joyce."

"*Merci a vous*," Joyce said, formal to the end.

There was a silence. There was always silence with Joyce. His silences, they said, were greater than the noise of his words, at least in his company, being present before the man, frail and human, unlike the writer, a Titan. She thought of telling him about Beckett's silences, too, but that seemed redundant. Joyce would have known about them better than Eileen did, and who is to say maybe Beckett's silences were a kind of homage of silence to the master of silence, Monsieur Joyce.

After a long silence Mr Joyce spoke. He summarized:

"Men regret their actions; women regret their failure to act.'

"A woman knows these things," Eileen said.

But Eileen did not mean that a woman knew regret for failing to act. What women knew—and Eileen being one of them—was when another woman had slept with their partners (broadly defined). Women regretting inaction and men regretting their actions had nothing to do with what Eileen believed what women knew.

She explained to Joyce who Miriam was. She was a young woman, young and beautiful and full of talent; she was South African, but she had become a part of Santiago's band while it toured in southern Africa. Eileen had had another fight with Santiago, storming off with some members of the band who were staying in a different hotel in Jo-burg, and Santiago had gone back to the other hotel.

"When I heard that Miriam had died, I suddenly realized that she was the one."

"The one?"

"I am not talking about her fucking my husband," she said.

"What are you talking about, Lovely?"

"She infected him," Eileen told him.

"The poxie?"

"No, worse," Eileen said.

"Crabs, lice, bedbugs, the heebie-jeebies, what, Lovely?"

She explained to Joyce how she had confronted Santiago in the lobby of the Hotel Lenox after they had received news from South Africa of Miriam's death. It was only a few days ago.

"Admit it," she said. "You slept with her."

"I am sad to hear of Miriam's death," Santiago said.

The Santas had been sat in the café near the hotel, drinking a cup of tea (Eileen) and a *petit dejeuner* coffee for her husband (Santiago). A letter had come in the mail from South Africa, addressed to Santiago. He was dying, but you would not know it to look at him. In the flesh he was still handsome and energetic, and you sensed being in the presence of a great musician. But by the end of the day, after he had done the early set from 6:30 at night until just before 9 o'clock in the evening, his energies flagged; he would become sluggish and bent, frail and needy. Eileen witnessed it nightly; a once-independent man, he had become dependent upon the kindness of his wife, even after she realized, time and again, that her husband deserved no kindness from her.

Sober now, and living in Paris for several years, their having lived in Algiers was but a memory, and their flight from there to Marseilles and later Bern and eventually Paris was just another story they told people when they were sat in the local cafes, practicing the Parisian version of *dolce far' niente.*

Eileen described herself as a *flaneur*; Santiago said that he was a miracle, plain and simple.

She liked to write in her notebook, read the newspapers, and watch the human parade go by, while Santiago wrote down musical notes on napkins and miscellaneous pieces of paper, smoked cigarettes if anyone had them—he would not buy them himself—drink strong espressos, also read the newspapers—the *International Herald Tribune* still his favorite, though it got shorter and shorter and more expensive by the minute, and more and more looked and read like the *New York Times*—and called people on his mobile telephone or told a coterie of young actors and musicians, artists and writers about his various adventures in Algiers or further south into Africa, the specter of the CIA or some other black ops Americans shadowing his physical and creative lives.

Honesty was a new principle in their lives. They had been dishonest with each other a long time; it was a wonder they were still married, Eileen thought, given all the deceptions they had promulgated upon each other. Drugs and alcohol will do that to a couple. If Eileen didn't exactly need Santiago, he most certainly needed her, and she thought of her obligations to him, not just as a husband—fuck that shit—but as a fellow human being who had these long and shared experiences with her, starting from their earliest days in North Africa, the Maghreb, specifically Algiers.

The French had a certain envy of this couple. They had lived in Algeria long after nearly all French people had been thrown out. He was a jazz musician, still nearly an almost mythical profession for anyone in Paris. She was a poet, a fierce Celt. French poets and essayists wrote about her cascading tendrils of red hair, her prominent nose—never a liability in France—and her piercing green eyes, her height, her thinness to the point of disappearing when she stood sideways. His resemblance to Albert Camus was noted in newspapers, one even calling him the black Camus of jazz, an expression that sounded far better in French than English. Besides being handsome still and an elder statesman of jazz, Santiago was a clothes horse, and the fashion magazines loved to write about what he was wearing when out and about the city.

Santiago was in his sixties; Eileen, in her forties. For several years, going to meetings, staying away from drugs and alcohol, they had been collectively and individually addressing the wreckage of the past, then jettisoning it. They lived comfortably in Paris, had money and prestige. At least, Santiago did. Eileen still struggled with who she was and what her purpose was in this life. Was she a poet and writer or was that something she did when she was young? Poetry had come back to her later in life. Her clairefontaine notebooks were filled with poems, most of which had been written at these café tables. Back home in their hotel room at the Lenox, she typed up the poems on her laptop. Her poems were being published in little magazines, mostly online ones in America. There was talk about one press or another doing a collection of her poems, which would be her first book in over twenty-five years. Eileen was writing essays too, about Algeria, Africa, their long exile, the wear and tear of being detached from America and Ireland for so long. Santiago had not seen his daughter in decades; Eileen did not even know her nieces and nephews, not to mention their progeny, making her a great-aunt to these unknown relations.

Santiago was active with his music, performing nightly,

recording regularly, doing interviews, making plans to release new work. A lawyer had been unraveling the byzantine affairs of his royalties in America; a European record company planned to release, once a month for the next five years, the complete catalogue of his works.

But then reality crept back into their café conversations.

Eileen had been badgering him again, as he called it, about Miriam.

"I was close with Miriam," Santiago said.

"You fucked her," Eileen stated.

"We spent the evening together after you stormed off to the other hotel where the band was staying in Jo-burg."

"Like I said," Eileen went on. "You fucked her."

Eileen had become a broken record when they went to the café. She could not stop asking him about Miriam. It was as if she were there when Miriam and Santiago went back to the hotel. The young woman had an exquisite jazzy African voice, Miriam did. He fixed her a drink. They sat on the couch. He began to flick through channels absent-mindedly. The whiskey did not taste good, but he liked the effect it had upon him and her. Suddenly he forgot about the fight he had with his wife Eileen (fuck her, he thought), and he relaxed enough to feel an erotic pull towards Miriam. He slid over towards her and she did not seem to mind. She was probably twenty-three years old, give or take a year or two either way. He was nearly sixty years old, a world famous jazz musician, but exiled from his country (the U.S.) because of his politics and the generally bad way that Americans treated black men particularly, whether they were rich and famous or poor and unknown.

"There is no justice," Santiago said. "None whatsoever."

But all this was conjecture, mere fiction.

No one knew how he got the virus. He may have gotten it from a dirty needle in Tangier.

Yet again they were sat at a table outdoors in a nearby café.

To the world, for all the world, they looked like a Parisian ideal. For all the world, to all the world, she looked like somebody you'd want to know if you were in Paris.

He still cut an attractive figure, smartly dressed, with an athletic build, socially engaging, articulate, angry, his eyes dark and piercing, a powerhouse of music, a legend, as they say, he put his arm around Miriam's shoulders, and she did not resist him. Instead, she gave into him, let him know how pliant she was encircled by his arms. Eileen, at least, knew the drill. His looks had not faded. He had the slightest touch of gray in his hair, just around his ears, and the only wrinkles on his face were around his eyes when he smiled. He was still built like an athlete, even though he didn't really do any exercise other than walking and later in the day performing on the stage. Had he not pursued music, he certainly might have been a famous athlete, though one who was now retired and enjoying the good life. At Columbia University, he had played basketball, but music exerted a greater pull than sports. There were very few black students in those days, but the university was in Harlem, so the streets around the university were filled with the people he most identified with, the brothers and sisters of Morningside Heights, and if he looked out his dorm window at night, he could see Harlem down below the Heights, vibrant and alive with music and culture, especially the jazz that was being made in Harlem. Jazz was the language of the neighborhood, and 125th Street was nothing but jazz, the same for Amsterdam Avenue, even Riverside Drive up around the university had a vibrancy that one associated with jazz. Duke Ellington lived on Riverside and 106th Street; the neighborhood was filled with lesser known but also prominent and influential jazz greats.

"We don't know that Miriam gave me the virus," Santiago said.

They were arguing with one another in the lobby of the hotel where they lived.

"But we know that you fucked her."

"Okay, I fucked her," he admitted.

It was the first time he admitted it.

He told Eileen: "This isn't going to help me get rid of the virus, and it's not going to bring back Miriam, an amazingly talented woman."

"You bastard," Eileen said, stomping off, going outside, where it was raining, then coming back into the lobby of the Lenox.

"I'm sorry," he said.

Eileen looked as if she was going to slug him.

"I'm sorry I ever met you."

"Is there anything I can do to make amends?"

"Keep your dick in your trousers," Eileen shouted.

People looked up from their French newspapers or their fat tomes of *Being and Nothingness*, their maps of Paris and their tourist guidebooks.

Eileen was sat at a café table just inside the club where Santiago nightly performed.

Santiago drew Eileen out of the café and the lobby of the hotel and went walking with her, back to their favorite café a few blocks away.

It was a warmish winter day, people in overcoats and puffer jackets, mufflers and scarves, wearing leather gloves and boots. But it was not so cold that they couldn't all be sitting outside, enjoying the sunlight.

He ordered an espresso, and the waiter nodded. Eileen ordered tea. Again, the waiter nodded, already knowing what the Santas usually had this time of day.

The waiter went off to fill the order.

With her hands resting on the table, Eileen put her head into them, and she wept like a baby.

"I'm sorry," Santiago said, rubbing her back, but she did not wish to talk to him any further.

Moments later she dried her eyes and stood to go again, reminding him that they needed to get back to the hotel. He had a 6:30 gig in the hotel café.

"What about our drinks?" he asked.

"Fuck the drinks," she said. "Tell the waiter something came up."

He called back the waiter and explained that they had to leave.

They stood and walked off, arm in arm.

"*C'est Santiago Santa*," one of the café customers said, as they faded into the distance.

It was a friend of Eileen's from her graduate school days in America who told the Santas that they were no longer on any FBI lists, for certain not on a Most Wanted list as they had once been in the 1970s, but then again not really welcome back in the U.S. The murder in Oakland for which Santa was deemed an accessory had long ago been vacated by the courts as being unsafe. The murder charges that were brought against several Oakland Black Panthers (Billy Williams and Jelly Roll Smith) were considered to be figments of the Oakland law enforcement's collective imagination. The two Panthers who were ultimately convicted of the crime were friends of Santa's, but not close ones. Twenty years later, in the 1990s, their convictions were thrown out. Still, Santiago did not wish to return to America after so many years away. But he did begin to make contact with people in his business— musicians, producers, financial people. Of the latter, through a copyright attorney, he began to receive royalty checks again, in some cases, more than twenty years past due. That is how Eileen and Santiago managed to afford doctors, dentists, treatments, the clothes in their closets, and were able to pay for their expensive hotel room, even with the heavy discount management gave them because he was the resident piano player in their tiny café off the lobby. People came to Paris to interview him and would go to the club at the hotel to hear him play. Eileen was his manager, juggling appointments with journalists, producers, other musicians, and dealing with fans, most of whom were older Europeans. It was in Europe where his reputation was in the realm of mythology. These fans were respectful of his time and energy, and besides, Paris was the kind of place where people, even if they knew who you were, tended to leave you alone, to respect your privacy. Everyone seemed to understand that Santiago was in his own endgame. His energy was finite, his time was running out. Like a character in a Beckett story, he would go on, but for how much longer no one knew, not even Eileen or Santiago himself. Eileen, being finely attuned to his ways, had the best sense of time as it applied to her husband. Like the cartoon prophets with long beards, wearing sandals and flowing gowns and carrying placards about the End Is Nigh, Eileen knew things that no one else knew. At night, she knew that Santiago Santa was frailer, and after he performed for a few hours, doing two sets from 6:30 to 9 o'clock in the evening, he got up from the piano, looked around for Eileen, and let her guide him to their room where he fell upon the bed in his clothes and instantly was asleep, not waking until morning.

"I cannot believe my good fortune," Miriam said. "I always dreamed of singing with you one day."

"Now you have," he said.

"Can I tour with you?"

Santiago said nothing.

He stared off a thousand yards. Finally he spoke:

"You are a very good singer, Miriam."

"Thank you," she said.

"I see a great future for you."

"I feel it is my destiny, Santiago."

He drank more whiskey. He channel-surfed. He put on some music, some South African music. It rang through the room, jazzy but really more pop.

Miriam shook her body in a dance, even though they still sat on the couch.

"I love this song," she said.

She stood and danced in front of Santiago.

"Come here," he said, and she did.

Living in Paris, Santiago's health did not improve, but nor did it get worse for many years. There was a stasis in which his life hung suspended. He floated through the world, at peace, but not entirely well. Living at the Hotel Lenox was good for him. He looked frail and shrunken, and yet when he sat down at the piano, his aches and pains disappeared. He looked like the Santiago Santa of the 1960s, only with graying hair and those wrinkles around his eyes. Eileen's outlook was a lot better than his own. She did not gain weight or suddenly stop being pale, and yet her vitality improved. His demeanor became less cynical, "less confrontationally Black," he said to her, "I'm not waking up with a grudge, with a chip on my shoulder, I'm feeling more peaceful." The two of them were regularly at the English-speaking AA meetings in Paris. Eileen really got into it, she said, "I never knew I had that spiritual gene like my mother." She took on sponsees after she got a few years of sobriety under her belt. Santiago went to the meetings and had coffee afterwards with people, but he didn't take to the slogans and the so-called "literature," a word which made him laugh. "A bunch of clichés," he said. But he would go to the meetings, usually five a week, and the two of them tried to support each other with the program. "Progress not perfection," she told him. He grimaced and complained, but with a hint of humor, "I married my mother."

"I guess I have the God gene too," Eileen said.

Santiago had something too, only he was hard pressed to say what it was.

His music changed in the 1990s during those final years in Paris. He mellowed. There was less anger in his music. There was no more "No Justice / No Peace" of the 1960s. Santiago had more acceptance of where it was his life's journey had taken him, from musical sensation as a young man, through those angry years in the Sixties, to those twenty years of exile in Northern Africa, all because of a trumped up police report in Oakland.

There were new generations of music lovers who didn't even know who Santiago Santa was, and now were getting to hear his music as if for the first time. The Santiago Santa they knew was this mellow older man, the elder statesman, dapper and frail, articulate as hell, speaking a different kind of truth than the angry brother of the 1960s. He was now a guy who played the piano in the café at the Hotel Lenox in Paris six nights a week, the early sets, when he usually went home right after the set, back upstairs to his room, where he read in bed until he turned off the light around ten at night. Mondays he had off.

Miriam kissed Santiago on the forehead, and he pulled her down and kissed her on the mouth.

"Take off your clothes," he said. "We have so little time together."

"You take off yours," she answered back.

He did, and then she did.

They were on a rug on the floor, him in his underwear and her in her underpants. She put her hands over her breasts until he said he wanted to see them, and she let go. Her breasts were big and shapely and he held them and kissed them and that seemed to set her off in the right direction. His hand was inside her underwear, rubbing her erect, as was he after she touched him, held his cock in her hands, then in her mouth, and then inside of her.

They made love on the floor between the sofa and the television.

Afterwards, she said she had to go. She wanted to give the money she earned for the concert to her mother. A brother was ill. It would help them enormously.

Santiago tried to give Miriam more money, but she refused.

"I am not a prostitute," she said. "I am a lover."

He laughed. She was right.

"Will you take me on tour?" she asked again.

"Let me think about it."

"I could leave with you tonight."

"I'll get back to you. I have to speak to my manager."

"Is that your wife?"

He was silent, then said yes, it was his wife.

Eileen still tried to fit a narrative around her life, of how the pieces and strands fit together—or not. One thing was certain: in Bern, the Santas had thrown in the towel. Neither could see straight, walk without wobbling, talk without sounding as if it were gibberish. In detox, they were separated from each other. But that lasted only a fortnight, as the staff slowly got them off the various drugs and alcohol concoctions that had fueled their lives. During the rehab, which lasted three months, they did not sleep together, but would see each other during the day, between their therapy sessions in group or the one-on-one sessions with a psychologist or addiction therapist. They ate their meals together, but with other patients. There was no privacy, no intimacy. Sometimes they found themselves in the same therapy session, late in the afternoon, or later in the day when they were allowed to mingle in a lounge area before the evening meal, they would sit in a corner away from the other patients, and catch up with each other. At night, they were separated again, the men in their dorm, the women in theirs. It cost

$75,000 a month, so the entire process cost the Santas $450,000, plus another hundred thousand in various medical procedures. But the real costs were not monetary but his health. Luckily, Santiago was recording again and now receiving royalties thanks to a lawyer in London who proved in court that Santiago had not received royalties for over twenty years. They came out of Bern free of substance abuse, though some of their medical treatments would need to continue in Paris. Eileen had hepatitis; Santiago was diagnosed with hepatitis and also was HIV-positive. He was put on an expensive regimen of retroviral drugs; she had to go on a long, painful Interferon treatment, at the end of which Eileen Coole was diagnosed as put paid to the old hep problem. Santiago's treatment would be ongoing for the rest of his life, however long he lived.

Before Miriam left, they embraced a long time at the door, kissing again. Miriam was beautiful, purply black and statuesque, and, man, she could sing, and she danced, and now Santiago knew that she could also make love. If he could find a place for her in the Santa group, he would do that. But he had to speak with Eileen and the other band members, some of whom had other African singers lined up for this tour. Once Miriam left the hotel room, Santiago thought about other things. It was not as though he dropped Miriam; she just slid away from his mind as he focused on the next bit of business in this long tour through Africa. Tomorrow they had to travel to Kenya by plane. It was an early flight that he had to be ready for.

He fell asleep on the couch, in his underwear, without brushing his teeth or doing anything else, waking in the morning with a hangover and a terrible taste in his mouth that he couldn't seem to shake even as he rode, alone, to the Johannesburg airport. Eileen and the others were there, waiting for him. The business of the tour came up right away, and that is what they talked about until they boarded their flight for Kenya. By the time the plane landed in Nairobi, Santiago and Eileen were talking to each other again. He had already forgotten about Miriam, especially after he met the next singer to join the group, her name Betty, and, yes, she could sing, she was beautiful, everyone loved her, and the band urged him to take her with them on the tour. He said that he would give it serious thought.

In Nairobi, Santiago apologized to Eileen for their fight, and she did the same. Neither asked the other about the people they had gone off with the night before. Eileen did not think of herself as anyone special just because she was Santiago Santa's wife. The wife was the last one to think about in his world; her job as manager of the group gave her far more clout in that world, and so she got down to the business of the bottom line, about how to keep the group in the black and not the red, how to make some money out of the tour, and especially how to make the promoters pay Eileen their fees up front because if she waited until after the concert, invariably they did not get paid the full amount they were due. At the new hotel in Nairobi, they kissed and made up.

In Paris, the Santas liked to go to a small café nearby to eat or have tea; Santiago used to smoke a cigarette after breakfast, but he stopped smoking at the rehab in Switzerland. Well, he stopped buying cigarettes, because he still smoked, mooching them from people in the café or out on the street or after a meeting. At least once a week, sometimes more, he saw a doctor of one kind or another. He had mouth sores, spots on his skin, shakes and vomiting: the usual crap one suffers with HIV, even with the illness in abeyance with the retroviral drugs, his immune system didn't seem to operate in an optimal fashion. Eileen's version of a health crisis was that old Irish curse of bad teeth and gums. Teeth were pulled; bridges were built; partials were calibrated by the taking of dental molds. She had several years of going to a periodontist. Every day the Santas walked around Paris for several hours, very slowly, stopping to look in shops, going to museums, eating lunch at a restaurant near the hotel, taking in the bookshops, coming home with books in French, Italian, Spanish, and English. There was no space left in their hotel room for books, so once they were read, they were given away. The only other things they bought were clothes and shoes. Eileen stuck with short leather jackets, jeans, dark sweaters (jumpers, she called them), and scarves. She had Frye boots shipped from the U.S. Santiago got into looking like a Parisian. He bought Mephisto shoes, so many that Eileen had to give away many pairs just to make room for the new ones.

He wore corduroy trousers or red chinos or expensive French jeans. Because he was often cold, he purchased jumpers (sweaters, he called them), turtle necks, some of them cashmere to keep warm. He liked coats that resembled safari jackets, filled with pockets that he, in turn, filled up with notebooks, pens, books, diaries, and maps. These safari jackets came in suede, cotton, nylon, and wool, depending upon the season, and with decidedly European understatement. He wore a beret; only Santiago Santa could get away with wearing a beret in Paris. He also wore Greek fisherman hats, Panama hats in summer, skull caps that he ordered from Northern Africa, and Londonesque scally caps.

All of what they had built together in Algiers was gone in one night: the next afternoon they were in Marseilles, where the ship docked. Marseilles was loud, dirty, corrupt, crowded, where Algiers, across the Mediterranean, a world away, had been something of an idyllic repast, despite the Islamic tensions, despite the martinets in power, despite the lack of freedom that most people in Algeria had. Both places were streaming with humanity, and they both had that in common. It was in Bern that it hit them at the same time that everything they owned was back in Algeria, never to be seen again.

Sometime after the Nairobi concert, Santiago caught what he thought was the flu. After a week in bed, he developed sores in his mouth. His doctor did not do a blood test, so it was dismissed as fatigue and flu, nothing more than that. He continued to drink heavily and to use drugs recreationally, as he put it, and it was difficult to say whether his overall health had declined. He was getting older; he was in his sixties. He had been gigging all over Africa, Eastern Europe, China, the Koreas, and Japan all his adult life. He was tired. He was just a little bit tired. He needed some rest.

Miriam died of AIDS a few years after they arrived in Paris. They heard about it from some African musicians passing through on their own whirlwind tour. She had performed with a jazz group up until the last six months of her life. Her death was fast and merciful and from pneumonia.

Eileen's resentments, mostly about Santiago's former infidelities in Africa, ebbed away, and in their place, she tried to forgive, and some days were better than others; she tried to treat it all like doing service, helping others, doing what she was told to do in order to stay sober, to remain clear—to stay clean—of drugs and alcohol. It wasn't always easy. The French had a way of making a bottle of wine seem like an essential part of a meal or even like an essential part of life. Those were the days when she pushed the Pause button; she would try to wade through the morass of her mind, getting to the other side. Some days it worked beautifully, and at night Eileen would put her head on the pillow and fall asleep immediately, without an ounce of self-pity or resentment, without a note of anger to propel her into the world of her dreams.

Other days Eileen did not seem capable of getting out of her own way, days in Paris when everything seemed like an affront or a slight, the world unfairly demanding that she give of herself without getting anything in return. She considered herself fortunate to have more days where helping Santiago felt like its own reward, when she would look back on the day and feel blessed to be alive, to be in Paris, to be able to help him in his final years on this Earth. Sometimes she was neither resentful nor grateful, but just alive in her own skin, no saint, no sinner, she was just more human, and the two of them went to the daytime meetings at the American church. There was something about going to a meeting with Santiago that lifted her spirits—that sent her forth into the rest of the day in a very upbeat way. Santiago would speak to the young guys in attendance, actors, writers, musicians—he was a kind of wise man to them, even though, at the time, he was only a few years sober himself. He never talked about his HIV anymore. Instead he talked to newcomers, asking how they were, so that even though he professed to find meetings "happy-clappy," as he called it, "nevertheless," Eileen would say, "you are more enthusiastic than I am." He would bring these newcomers with them when they went off to have coffee, a meeting after the meeting, they called it.

Sometimes he ate some food, a sandwich, or had a soup, telling everyone he was dying for a cigarette or even a drink, but that he would have neither *today*. "Tomorrow," he said, "who knows? Maybe tomorrow I will have a drink. Today? I'm all right today. Today I'm not going to drink anything stronger than this coffee." He then drank from his espresso cup, savoring the strong flavor. Then he mooched a cigarette from one of the young men who idolized him, and he walked away from the table and smoked his cigarette near the curb. One of these young guys, a newcomer, an actor, an American from New York, his name Billy, asked Santiago about performing at Muhammad Ali's "Rumble in the Jungle." "It must have been great being there," Billy said to Eileen. She remembered Santiago going off with another woman, some African goddess from Kinshasa. "I wouldn't know," she said. "Ask the man." Santiago sipped his coffee and thought. "I didn't treat Eileen well during that time." She said: "That's an understatement." "I'm sorry," he said. It was the first time he said that and he seemed to really mean it; it was not just a knee-jerk response to get himself off the hook. She acquiesced in the face of his apology. "Is this a Step Nine or a long, drawn out Step Ten?" she asked. He laughed, then to Billy, Eileen said: "We were all high as kites." "And Ali?" the young actor from New York asked. "Ali was great," Santiago told him. "He was a great boxer and a great human being. I loved Ali. He would inflict upon George Foreman one of the most psychologically brutal and exacting strategic defeats in the history of boxing. He drew Foreman in like a mongoose draws in a cobra, with trickery and deceit. Amazingly, Archie Moore, I think, was working George's corner, and Archie's nickname was 'The Mongoose,' and yet that day the Mongoose was in

Angelo Dundee's corner in the shape of Muhammad Ali. By Round Eight, you could turn Foreman over. He was done."

Eileen walked down the stairwell at the Lenox. Joyce appeared. He said: "You know how I feel about redheaded women." Eileen nodded. "They buck like goats," she said. "Yes, they do," he answered, "and you have been an excellent student of my work." "We are all in the penumbra of your long shadow." He smiled. "I have caused a lot of mischief in my day and apparently long after that day. Now tell me more about that poxie slag your beau had been *schtooping*." "There is nothing to say, Mr. Joyce, but she was not a poxie slag. She was a singer." "I love singers," he said, changing his attitude completely. Eileen did not engage this incorporeal matter because Joyce was sincere, but rather because he wasn't sincere at all. He was a chameleon, changing his colors and shapes at a moment's whim. He was the master not only of prose but of deception. He was the ultimate Jesuit, and in that sense, he was Jesuitical before he was anything else. Eileen didn't care; in fact, she preferred that they interacted this way. Of singing he said: "I was one myself. A tenor. The Irish tenor. I rivalled the great John McCormick." He sang a riff of "Danny Boy." Then he spoke of

Londonderry air
London derriere

Ah! he sighed, pleased with these results, though it was hard to effect a pen and paper in this incorporeal state. He went on: "Sometimes I see you with this dark fellow whom I have been calling St. Augustine." "That's Santiago Santa," Eileen corrected him. "A handsome devil," he said. "Devil is right." "Has he been unkind to you?" "He has been unkind to himself. He's not well." "Is it the head?" "No, it is not the head." "The heart?" "No, not that either. He's sick in his body." "The pox?" "He's got a virus." "They are tricky," he said. "I once studied to be a doctor. What I don't know about medicine could fill a book." "Is it *Ulysses*?" "Redheaded women buck like goats," he said, "and their tongues are as sharp as the razor's edge."

Eileen told Joyce that her own diseased brain had set up these obsessive scenarios in her head. She could not stop seeing Santiago taking Miriam to that other hotel in Jo-burg, plying her with whiskey—they were all still drinking back then—and fucking the pants off of her on the rug in front of the couch of the suite they had rented. She explained that she had chosen to stay at the hotel with the musicians that night and did not go home with him. He went back to their hotel with Miriam.

"The singer?" "Yes, the singer." "Opera?" "No, jazz." "Ma Rainey," he said. "Yes, though more bop." "Bop? Bop? What, tell me, is bop?" "It's American," she said. "Ah," Joyce said. "Charlie Parker, he came along right after you popped the mortal coil. He invented bebop in Harlem." "Well, I know Harlem," Joyce said. "It used to be filled with Irish saloons." "She was more like Billie Holiday." "I don't know this name," Joyce said. "When was she singing?" "In the forties." "Ah," he sighed. "I was with the ancestors by then. I drank myself to death on white wine, Lovely." "She was the best there ever, Billie was." "I believe you." "Listen," Eileen said, whipping out her mobile telephone and calling up Holiday's "Strange Fruit." Joyce was practically in tears. "Such purity of expression," he said. "So Irish, in a way." "She was part Irish." "Ah," he said.

Before he disappeared back into the walls of the hotel, Joyce told Eileen a joke: "What do you call a woman whose one leg is shorter than the other."

She shrugged, unsure of an answer.

"Eileen," he said, and disappeared.

THE PRODIGAL DAUGHTER

At the time of her mother's death, Eileen had called her once a week from London. She even wrote the odd letter now and then, getting into a correspondence with the old one. They made promises to meet, and her mother reminded Eileen that the old woman (herself) was not long for the mortal coil. It was now or never. So Eileen booked a flight to Dublin and came over one weekday morning in November. Her mother asked Eileen to take her to Clare, where the mother was from, and Eileen agreed, renting a car at the airport before she drove over to Sandymount, where her family's house had been for generations. They packed a small valise with clothes and a lunch basket to sustain them in the journey, and lit out of Dublin for the frontiers of the west.

Her mother wanted to go to the usual places a tourist might visit, so it was not so much a sentimental journey to her mother's childhood haunts as it was a trip to the Cliffs of Moher and an afternoon exploring the Burren. The Cliffs were crowded with tourists, even in November, so they purchased a few trinkets from a traveler girl, and then went on their way. At the Burren, they lingered much longer, and when the chill wind dug far into them, they sought shelter in the rental car, which was small enough that it almost felt like it might lift off the ground from the force of the wind.

From her handbag, Eileen's mom surprised her

daughter with a copy of one of Seamus Heaney's books.

"I didn't know you read poetry," Eileen said.

"There's a lot about me you don't know," her mother said.

Her mother read Eileen a poem about being at the sea in Clare.

"This poem," her mother said. "This poem is the reason I wanted to come here."

Eileen didn't want to disappoint her mother and tell her that the poem was Eileen's least favorite of Seamus' poetry.

After the poem was read, they sat in silence. The Irish were good with their silences. Then her mother cleared her throat.

"It's sentimental," her mother said. "But I like it. I like it the way one likes a greeting card or a popular song that is sentimental."

Eileen listened to the wind whipping around outside. It was as if she were playing Cordelia to her mother's King Lear.

"His later work is sentimental," her mother went on. "It's the early work that counts."

"I didn't know you liked poetry, mother."

"When you become an OAP, you have to do something with your time. I take the odd class or two, Introduction to Poetry, the Poetry of Ireland, stuff like that. It fills the time."

"Why?" Eileen asked, being a kind of itinerant journalist, poet, and philosopher herself.

"I thought it would help me to understand yourself and the work you do."

"Did," Eileen said. "I haven't published a proper book in donkeys' years."

"Now don't spoil the view with a shedload of self-pity, Eileen Coole, there is no need for that out here on the Burren where we are more pagan than Christian and more two women than a mother and child."

"I'm sorry," Eileen said. "Usually I'm a bit more sanguine."

"You were quite the emotional bundle of goods as a child."

"Don't let's get into me childhood, ma."

"Luckily I can't remember a thing about it anymore," her mother said.

Behind them, the Burren receded, its craggy shore, its colorful weeds, its winds, drifted out of sight in the rearview mirror of the rental car. It looked like it did a million years ago, before history. The only one to age was Eileen. Her mother looked as she had when Eileen was a girl. Her mother was a woman of perpetual middle age, even in old age. She had her rosy cheeks and disposition; her plaid wool skirt like a third-rate royal; her silk scarf tied around her head, and her waterproof overcoat of cotton and synthetic cloth. She wore her sensible shoes. She had been the doctor's wife most of her long life, and then she had been the doctor's widow, a grandmother, an old friend to her neighbors, a church lady, and even a writer of left-wing political ideas to the local newspapers.

All in all, she was not a bad mam, and that was her life, as she appeared to be at the end of it now.

They spent the evening at a B & B in Ennis. In the early morning, they drove into town so that her mother could attend Mass. They came back afterwards to the B & B and ate a light breakfast before driving back to Dublin that morning, taking turns at the wheel.

As Eileen drove, her mother pointed to the dimpled marks on her daughter's freckled arms.

"What is that?"

"What?"

"Those indentations."

"Tracks," Eileen said.

"Tracks?"

"From shooting up," Eileen told her. Then she said: "I don't know."

"Heroin?"

"For fuck's sake, ma, I'm seventy-fucking-years old."

"You wasted your life with that man," her mother said.

"He's dead."

"I'm at death's doorstep meself, girl. I'm ninety-five years around the sun. We have to talk. No husband, no children. You're all alone in London. If you collapsed in front of the British Library, people would just step right over you, Eileen. There is no family there, no friends. You are all alone. Isn't it time you came home?"

"For fuck sake, ma."

"That man took you from your family, your world, for what, to turn you into a drug addict."

"I'm clean now," Eileen said. "That was years ago."

"What did you have in common with a Cuban man?"

"His mother was Irish," Eileen said. "That was the attraction. I reminded him of his mother. That's all men want, they want their mother."

"I was not at all like your father's mother, Eileen Elizabeth."

"Don't kid yourself, ma."

"Your father loved me for who I was," her mother said.

"Bloody fucking hell," Eileen shouted. "I just missed the turn. Let me concentrate on the driving."

Once Eileen got them back on the right road to Dublin, the car fell silent for a time, and a sort of peace descended upon them. But then Eileen felt the urge to clear the air.

"Santiago was born in Brooklyn," she said. "That's how I became a US citizen too, once we married."

"Did he even love you?"

"He loved me all right," Eileen said. "But love isn't always a blessing."

"I've listened to his music," her mother said. "He was very good at what he did."

Eileen had spent a lifetime away from her family and Ireland. They did not know her anymore. Assumptions had been made about her, and then calcified. She was not going to change all of that after seventy years with one drive to the west of Ireland or one afternoon on the Burren.

She was clean now, and hadn't been high in nearly three decades. She did not want a medal, and yet why didn't they see her progress the way others saw it. The arc of her life now bent towards life and away from the destruction of her addictions, all those years that she and Santiago lived in the Maghreb and travelled the world giving concerts everywhere so long as it was not America.

They had toured Africa many times. She had met Nelson Mandela and Robert Mugabe, to mention two extremes, and they had toured in Russia and the Far East—China, Korea, Japan. They had even gone to North Korea for a concert because Kim Jong-Il loved Santa's music. She had shook the Great Leader's hand, which was soft and girlish and seemed to lack bones. He smelt of strong cologne, with an undercurrent of kimchee.

They had flown from Pyongyang to Beijing where Santa gave another concert. Then they flew to Tokyo, where he performed for a bunch of VIPs at a sleek, plush hotel in Raponggi. Next they went to Seoul. After that sold-out concert at the King Sejong Centre, they were approached backstage by some high-ranking State Department officials—some CIA spooks—two men and a woman.

The woman was a beautiful young Korean-American, and Eileen figured that her husband would be sleeping with the young official before they left South Korea. It was just the way it was in those days. No one knew he was HIV yet; maybe he was not even inhabiting the virus then. That may have happened later.

The two men did not flirt with Eileen, but looked at

her disapprovingly. She was wearing a kind of rock-chick velour suit of trousers and jacket in the color of radiant Titian blue, with a ruffly white linen shirt whose buttons seemed to have disappeared in transit. Eileen wore no bra, so that what chest she had was almost completely exposed to everyone. Her red hair was like Medusa's, big and curly and flopping about everywhere. Her green eyes rolled around in her head.

She heard the men talking to Santa about revoking his citizenship. For what? he asked. They did not answer. But the point was moot. He had not used his U.S. passport in years, preferring to travel using his Irish passport which he had from his mother's parents.

The younger man wore a tight-fitting blue suit, a white shirt, and red tie. His brogues were shined like two black coffins. The older man was a seasoned Asia hand or at least seemed to be one. He was quite tall, even towering over the very tall Eileen, and his face was long and craggy, like the mountains which surrounded the former imperial city they found themselves in. He was a career diplomat, she thought. His suit was blue with wide chalk gray pinstripes, his tie had some college insignia on it from Yale or wherever. The shirt was blue and button down, and he wore oxford loafers with bright red socks.

"I was born in America," Santiago said. "I have not broken any laws. Politically I don't see eye to eye with you. But that is not, in and of itself, a crime."

"When is the last time you paid your taxes, sir?" the craggy one asked.

"I stopped paying taxes in response to the Vietnam War."

"That was a long time ago, sir."

"The arc of history is long," Santiago said.

"But it bends towards justice," Eileen piped in.

"Who's she?" the tall Asia hand asked.

"Wife," Santa said.

"Wife?"

"Yes, that's Eileen Santa there."

Eileen bowed.

Mr. State Department sneered at her.

"Is she an American?"

"You'd have to ask her," Santa said.

"Are you an American, mam?"

Eileen smiled at him.

She was very high that night.

"I'm asking you a question, mam. Are you an American?"

"She's Cathleen nee Houlihan," Santa said, getting into the goof.

There were hundreds of people standing around backstage at the Sejong Cultural Centre waiting to meet Santiago Santa, to shake his hand and tell him how much they loved his music. No one could get to him as long as the officials held him captive backstage.

"Mam, I've asked you a question several times now. Are you an American?"

Eileen's paleness, even then, was astonishing. There was no one in the room paler than she. She was so floppy that it seemed as if she had no muscles to support her long frame. She was not someone, though, who was easily intimidated, and besides she and Santa had been through the ringer with the US for years. Everywhere they went spies followed them.

She might look like a wispy pre-Raphaelite portrait, but Eileen Coole was as tough as they got. That's what Santa liked about her. She could handle anything.

"Miss Houlihan, you have the right to remain silent if you wish."

Eileen attempted to speak, but nothing came out. Words betrayed her. She felt the room spinning.

Earlier that day on the flight from China, she had drunk a bottle of Jameson's and topped it off with a lot of marijuana. She did a few lines of cocaine that a stagehand provided her. She also snorted some heroin. The bottle of Irish whiskey had come from Kim Jong-Il who had given it to Santiago as a present. No one but Eileen drank it, and it was long gone by the time the State Department people spoke to them.

Nothing more was remembered about the evening. Eileen woke up still drunk in her hotel room in downtown Seoul, and then the entourage grabbed a bunch of limos to take them to Kimpo Airport on the outskirts of the city. When Eileen came to again, they were on another 747 airline to a new country to perform.

"Where are we going?" she asked one of the technicians who travelled with the group.

Santa was somewhere else on the plane or on another

plane, probably with the Korean-American woman from the State Department. He might not agree with the official's politics, but that never stopped him from making love to someone.

"We're doing three shows in Manila," the techie said. He was a young guy, a very good sound man. He was bearded and long-haired, like a throwback to the hippie era. His home was around Detroit, where he had been a theatre director. His name was Forest. He had gone to Yale Drama School, and when the tour ended, he planned to open a fringe theatre in Detroit. Eileen slept with him that night. But she remembered almost nothing about it. It was not the first time this had happened with Forest, and it would not be the last.

They were in Manila for two days before Santa showed up a few hours before his first concert. He was high on heroin, reefer, and vodka, and was about as coherent as a snake. But everyone knew the routine, and he played especially well that night. The whole group did, but particularly their leader.

Eileen loved his music and the man, but after the concert she let her other feelings be known to Santa.

"I want a divorce," she said.

"What's this all about?" Santa asked.

"I want it now."

"In Manila?" he asked. "Isn't this a very Catholic country? I don't think they give divorces, even for you, Cathleen nee Houlihan."

"Fuck you, Santa," she said. "Fuck you and the horse you rode in on."

"It was a plane, Eileen. Are you all right?"

A month after Eileen visited her mother, the old woman took ill. One of Eileen's brothers—it was Dermott, the doctor—called her in London and booked her a flight over to Dublin. He had an intuition that their mother was not going to make it. Eileen arrived Thursday evening. The next day, their mother's cold turned into a wheezy chest and a cough. By Saturday it turned into pneumonia. Sunday she was coherent for a few hours, then lapsed in and out of consciousness. By Monday, her mother was dead. Eileen and two of her sisters, Maeve and Fionna, stood vigil around the sick bed, attending to their mother's final wishes. Before the mother expired, she spoke on Sunday morning to them, one sister older than Eileen, the other younger. A fourth sister lived in a cloister in Nova Scotia, Canada, and she was nowhere to be seen, nor would they be able to contact her that easily or to fly her home to Dublin, if her mother died.

"I'm so proud of all my girls," her mother told the three sisters who ranged in age from seventy-five to sixty. "But I'm especially proud of Eileen."

"Eileen?" Fionna asked.

"Who?" the younger sister Maeve said.

Eileen was speechless.

"What's so special about Eileen?" Fionna demanded.

Fionna had a point. She had cared for their mother almost daily in old age. Maeve was there after work, several times a week. They dumped bedpans, ironed sheets, took her for convalescent walks around Sandymount, spoon-fed her porridge, read to her from favorite books. All Eileen had done was to take their mother in her last month of life for a two-day outing to Clare.

Big deal.

"I'm so proud of Eileen," the mother said, "for a million things, including she got herself clean and sober, the first one in the family."

"She's the only one in the family who's an addict, ma," Maeve dead-panned.

"Eileen went to graduate school in America," her mother went on deliriously, speaking as if Eileen was not there. "She writes poetry, girls. She's a poet."

All of them spoke as if Eileen weren't there.

"For fuck sake," Fionna said.

"I wish you wouldn't talk that way," her mother said.

"Eileen bunked off from her doctoral program in California to shack up with some Cuban criminal who took her halfway around the world."

"That's a lie!" Eileen shouted.

"She's a common whore!" Fionna shouted back.

Their mother coughed.

A nurse came in and scolded them for the tensions they had created around their dying mother's bed.

Their mother wheezed and coughed and went in and out of consciousness from that point onwards, the clarity of her mind slowly oozing out of her tired body. That was the last of their mother's verbal pyrotechnics. From then on, their mother might wake, even smile, hold a hand, seem to whisper things, but nothing more was said. She never spoke again. The whisperings were false messages from the beyond, sounds upon the wind, bird calls.

"What about us?" Maeve asked no one. "She had seven children. Eileen's not the only one."

Sean, one of their brothers, had died in a car accident in his teens. Dermott became a doctor, like his father; Brian was the lawyer in the family. Their sister Maryjoe had become the cloistered nun in Canada.

"Look what you've done," Fionna said.

"Me?" Eileen asked.

"You've upset me mom," Fionna said. "We cared for her in old age. Wiping the oatmeal off her chin. Changing her adult nappies. Bathing her. Giving her sponge baths. What did you do, Eileen?"

"She wrote her a poem for mothering day," Maeve said.

"That was years ago," the oldest declared.

"It was years ago," Maeve agreed.

"I could have written that poem," Fionna said.

"Then why didn't you?" Eileen asked.

"You beat me to the punch."

They stood over their wheezing, dying mother, arguing with each other like they were children. In a sense, they still were. Each inhabited a space in the family that had been assigned quite early in life. Fionna was the caregiver; Maeve was a kind of after-thought.

"The Mistake," her siblings called her.

Eileen was not like the others – smarter at her studies, more creative, easy in her ways, never struggling in any subjects. Boys adored her, and so did girls at school. Teachers loved her clever answers. She was gifted, they said. By comparison, Fionna had been a figure of fun, slightly overweight, slightly less pretty than her younger sisters. Maeve had been too airy-fairy, not rooted to the earth the way Eileen had been. All of them could sing and play the piano, but Eileen had the purest voice and the surest hand on the piano.

Her sisters believed—despite the evidence to the contrary—that Eileen never struggled with anything. Even her rough times in North Africa and later in London added to the legend of Eileen Coole.

The sisters—all but the nun in Nova Scotia and Eileen—had married, had children, and raised these families, slowly taking them away from their aspirations, whatever they were, singing, dancing, acting, painting. Her sisters had married well. But none of them did the things of their youth anymore. They did not even attend plays or concerts unless it had something to do with their children's lives.

Prodigal Eileen gallivanted over the globe, sending them postcards from Egypt or Singapore, calling them every few years from Phnom Penh or Mumbai. She was drunk or high, her speech slurred, and what she said was repetitious and inane.

The family was about to settle down for a Christmas dinner, the goose just out of the oven, when Eileen called them from South America. She was with Santiago in Buenos Aires. Did any of them ever see a proper tango?

The steak in Argentina was beyond belief, she said. Eileen would say that, though. She was sending some very special soap home to their mother. Be on the lookout for her package.

"We all can't be Eileens," Fionna said at their mother's death vigil.

"I only want you to be yourself," Eileen told her big sister.

Her baby sister cried at the foot of the bed.

Eileen went over to comfort her, but Maeve pushed her away.

Fionna wet their mother's lips with a sponge. Their mother mouthed words, but nothing was intelligible, nothing was spoken ever again coherently. The unspokenness of death descended upon the hospital room, as the sisters dug in for the long night ahead.

Eileen had wanted to apologize to her sisters, but she did not know exactly for what, so she hung back.

She went and sat in a chair in the far corner as Fionna sponged their mother's lips again and Maeve cried at the foot of the bed.

Eileen, being the prodigal one, sat in the corner by herself.

London—Nice—Liznjan—Pula—Chicago, 2006-2021

M. G. STEPHENS (Michael Gregory Stephens) is author of over 30 books, including *The Coole Trilogy*, consisting of the novels *Season at Coole, The Brooklyn Book of the Dead*, and *Kid Coole.* His novel *King Ezra* (Spuyten Duyvil, 2022), has been translated into Italian as *Re Ezra.* In the recent past he has written such books as the hybrid work of poetry, fiction and fact, *History of Theatre or the Glass of Fashion* (MadHat Press, 2021), and the story collection *Jesus' Dog* (Paycock Press, 2024). Spuyten Duyvil will soon publish his linked stories, *Come On, Eileen*, and his long-awaited memoir *When Poetry Was the World*, about the early days of the Poetry Project in 1966. (He wrote a PhD on the Poetry Project at the University of Essex in Colchester, England from 2003 to 2006.) Stephens also continues to publish poetry in such books as *Sixmilebridge* (Spuyten Duyvil, 2023) and *Popeye, Unchained* (2025), a collaboration of 85 mostly unrhyming blank verse sonnets accompanied by 85 collages by Brooklyn artist Archie Rand.